a DOG and his GIRL MYSTERIES
MYSTERIES

1

Play DEAD

a DOG and his GIRL MYSTERIES

Play DEAD

Jane B. Mason
and Sarah Hines Stephens

SCHOLASTIC INC.

ISBN 978-0-545-43624-3

12 11 10 9 8 7 6 5 4 3 2   12 13 14 15 16/0

Printed in the U.S.A.   40
First printing, September 2012

The text type was set in Adobe Garamond Pro.
Book design by Elizabeth Parisi

For girls and their dogs, especially
Nora and Molly
Sarah and Daisy
Violet and Watson and Talulah

CHAPTER 1

I was under the table with my head on my girl's shoes. Her grassy, soapy, and slightly bacon-y smell drifted into my snout. Ah. I loved it under the table. I was hard to see there. I was nearly invisible. Undercover. Not an easy thing to pull off when you're a ninety-pound German shepherd.

And the other great thing? Even though I was hard to see, I could see just about everything. That included any bits of dinner that might "accidentally" fall. *Mmm*. Bits of dinner. I loved bits of dinner. Really, really loved bits of dinner. The only thing better was food I stole from The Cat.

The Cat's food was good. The actual cat? She drove me crazy. The Cat thought she could get away with anything. *Anything.* But I saw her crouching. I saw her twitching tail. I saw the uncovered butter dish on the counter. I gave a small "Whuff," to let her know I was watching. She didn't look at me. But she heard. "Whuff." Her tail stopped twitching.

Cassie heard, too. My girl's hand appeared under the table and she gave me a pat. "Easy, Dodge." I licked her hand. I was easy. Just keeping things in line. I licked again. She always tasted good, but tonight she tasted burger good. Burgers were for dinner. I loved burgers. Burgers were my favorite.

Cassie's hand disappeared and I had to duck fast. The Sister had a sneaker-swinging habit, and her sparkle-crusted shoes were coming close. Too close. I adjusted, putting one paw on either side of Cassie's Converse and leaning to one side.

With my head cocked I could hear better in my good ear. Under the table I could see *and* hear. And what I heard was The Sullivan pack having a meeting. The Mom was chewing her words before spitting them out. My hairs tingled. When The Mom chewed her words, it meant something. It meant she was working things over in her head. Two words kept repeating: *Verdel Ward*. It was a name. A name that was bugging The Mom like a bad burr.

In the Sullivan pack, The Mom was in charge. Sometimes The Dad took over, but not usually. Me? I only took orders from one human. The one who saved me. Cassie. Cassie would do anything for me, and I would do anything for her. But I'll admit I would seriously consider any request The Mom made. Yeah. I would sit for her if she asked. Maybe even roll over.

The Mom *used* to be in charge of me. When I was on the force, she was top dog — the Chief of Police. She gave *all* the orders. And still does — just not to me. I had to leave the force. But it wasn't because I wasn't good at my job. I was good. I'm still good.

I graduated top of my class from K-9 Academy. I was trained to notice *everything*. Like my girl's heart rate picking up. And her toes curling and uncurling beneath my chin. Cassie was great at noticing things, too. She was noticing right now.

My girl didn't have training, but she had something just as good. Instincts. We both smelled a case, and we kept sniffing. And listening.

There was a whole lot to listen to. Even The Brother. The whole pack was talking tonight.

Usually at dinner The Brother kept his feet pointed toward the door. He kept buzzing things in his ears to drown out the pack until The Mom told him to take them out. The Brother was a little over two in dog years. He had a bit of hair on his face, and his voice was getting growly. It was a hard time, two. I remembered. When you're two you wanted to leave the pack. But you didn't. But you did. But you didn't.

The Brother was chewing up the same two words as The Mom: *Verdel Ward. Verdel Ward. Verdel Ward.*

I licked my chops. The air tasted like burgers. I tried not to drool. Or fantasize about a plate sliding off the table and spilling food all over the floor. Food on the floor was mine, or The Cat's. Or mine. That was another reason I liked my under-the-table territory.

"Funny how everyone suddenly cares about the billionaire," The Mom said between bites. "It's not like Ward had many friends when he was alive."

"You mean *any* friends," The Sister said. Friends were important to her.

4

The Dad snorted in agreement. "Yup, I think employees and clients were the closest relationships he had — relationships where money changed hands."

"No doubt." The Brother surprised everyone with his talk. Even me. And he talked to me when nobody else was around. Sometimes when nobody else was around he talked a lot. "We trick-or-treated at Ward's house once. We thought maybe the richest guy in town would be giving away something *good*. All we got were chalky mints that weren't even wrapped! He was really cheap for a rich guy."

It was silent for two breaths. For The Brother this was a major howl. He shifted his feet. I pictured his face. Brown hair hanging into his brown eyes. Straight nose. Long face. Like an Afghan hound, only human.

"Ward was the richest man in town?" Cassie asked.

She was digging. Good girl.

The Mom was nodding — I could hear it. "Maybe even the state."

"That's because he never gave anybody a single penny," The Brother growled. Those mints had made him mad.

The Sister swung her feet faster. "I guess that's why everyone hated him."

5

Cassie's toes clenched and held under my jaw. Hated. Sometimes "hated" people didn't just die. Sometimes they were killed.

"Doesn't matter how much money you have when you're dead. You can't take it with you," The Dad said. He wanted everyone to be happy. Happy-making was a job for golden retrievers.

"I bet he wishes he *could* have taken it with him," The Brother said. "I bet he wishes he was stuffed in a coffin full of cash for all eternity."

"I half wish he could've taken it with him, too," The Mom sighed. "It's going to be a while before they know who gets his money, but that's not what's bogging us down at the station." The Mom trailed off, and I could tell the burr was burrowing in.

The Sister stopped chewing. She set her burger down. Was she done? No. She picked it up. She set it down. She wasn't done. She was annoyed. "Do we have to talk about creepy stuff at every meal?" she whined. "Can't we talk about —"

"I like hearing what's going on at the station." My girl cut her off. "Especially the weird stuff."

"Yeah, but coffins and dying and . . . ick." The Sister wiggled and tucked her toes over the rung of the chair.

"Ward didn't *have* a coffin to stuff money into," The Dad pointed out. "He didn't even have an urn."

"Huh?" Cassie shifted in her seat without moving my pillow foot. "What do you mean?"

I cocked my good ear toward The Dad. Yeah. What did he mean?

"You need a body for a coffin, and they never found Ward's," The Dad explained. He sounded disappointed. The Dad dealt with dead people every day. He was a coroner. He liked a body.

Then, whoom! Something flickered in the corner of my eye — a piece of burger bun falling to the floor! I got my mouth under it. Mmm. Ketchup and burger juice. *More?* I wondered crazily. *Please, please let there be more.* A beggy whine tried to get out of my throat.

"If they never found a body, how do they know he's dead?" Cassie acted like she didn't knock that piece of bun off the table on purpose. What a girl.

"He went for a swim off Tempest Point," The Mom explained. "It's considered an 'imminent peril' situation because there's no way he could survive in those waters for more than a few hours. So after four months his housekeeper filed a petition to have him declared dead."

"Tempest Point?" The Sister interrupted. "Isn't that where they have all those warning signs? Don't people drown?"

"That's the spot," Cassie said. "So Ward disappears in the sea, and now, after being hated by everybody, he suddenly has lots of friends?"

"His *money* has lots of friends," The Brother corrected. His fork clinked down. His plate was clean. Bummer.

The Mom tapped her foot. I remembered she sometimes forgot to eat when she was chewing on a case. The thought made me wag. *Burger. Burger. Burger.*

"Right. He doesn't have friends so much as people who want his money," The Mom said. "His housekeeper claims that thirty years of service is worth a cut of the fortune. And Mayor Baudry wants the Ward estate donated to the city. He says that he and Ward had had several off-the-record conversations about it. But I don't think Ward's ever had several conversations with anyone. And then this . . ." The Mom tapped her finger on the table. It was

8

a newspaper tap. Muffled. "The press reports that Ward had a long-distance girlfriend."

"No way," The Sister balked. "That's just weird."

"What's *weirder* is that Ward had no will," The Mom said.

I felt Cassie's toes unclench. She lifted the front of her foot a tiny bit. She sensed it before The Mom said it.

"I'm opening a full investigation," The Mom declared. The hesitation in her voice was gone. Her decision was made. As soon as the words were out of her mouth, she took a big bite of burger. But I was too excited to care. An investigation. A trail. Clues!

I thumped my tail on the floor to let Cassie know that I'd been listening.

My girl slipped the last few bites of her burger to me and I quickly took care of them. Nobody had to know. Then Cassie put her hand on my head and scratched *the* spot, the one behind my ears that makes me go limp. Her foot relaxed and so did I. I had everything I wanted. Burger. Girl. Case. *Woof.*

CHAPTER 2

I slid my last bite of burger to Dodge and got up from the table. I was on cleanup. Ugh. Why was I always on cleanup when I had a new case to mull over? I thought about asking Owen or Sam to switch dish nights with me, then questioned my sanity. Sam would never do a task she could put off, and Owen would probably just grunt in response. The only way to get out of the dishes was to get them done.

Swooping up a handful of silverware and adding it to my stack, I headed into the kitchen.

Dodge followed, and not just because there were burger drippings involved. Dodge and I were a team. We did almost everything together, and he was better company than anyone else in the house. "Can you believe I'm on dish duty?" I groused in his direction.

He gazed back at me, his liquid brown eyes full of sympathy. Then he lowered his head, put his paws down in play position, and let out a little bark like he does when he wants me to throw the Frisbee.

"I know, I know," I said. "We've got *real* work to do." I gave him a pet and went back to the dining room for another stack. Then I opened the dishwasher. It was full of clean dishes. "Owen, you forgot to unload the dishwasher again!" I shouted at the top of my lungs. Which maybe wasn't totally necessary, but felt good anyway.

Lately Owen was a problem. He didn't want anything to do with the rest of us anymore — especially me. Or at least that was how it felt. So even if I got him to come do his job, it wouldn't be fun. It wouldn't involve jokes and miniature water fights. Not like it used to.

Dodge thumped his tail on the floor, and I bent down so we were forehead to forehead. "Good idea," I told him as I ruffled his neck fur. "It'll be a lot faster." I put the plates on the floor so he could get to work on the prewash. "No water needed!" I boasted, feeling efficient *and* environmental as I started to unload the clean dishes.

By the time I finished the bottom rack, the plates on the floor had been licked clean and Dodge was lingering over the burger platter, his big pink tongue searching for that last bit of flavor. I grabbed the last few dishes, loaded them, and closed the dishwasher. "Time for the good stuff!"

I darted into the hall and hit the stairs just in front of Dodge, who passed me halfway up. "No fair! Four-leg advantage!" I called as we rounded the corner and shoved open the door to our room.

Unfortunately, it was also my sister's room — at least for a few more days. And there she was, Samantha the spectacular, sitting in our swivel chair with her sparkly shoes parked on our desk, dangerously close to a stack of innocently bystanding mysteries. "Ahem," I said.

Sam didn't even acknowledge me — she just kept nodding her sandy blonde bob, petting her cat, Furball, and leafing through her copy of *Seventeen*. I was about to get huffy when I realized she was plugged into her iPod. Annoying, but it explained not listening to me. That, and the fact that she was generally too busy listening to *herself*.

I ran my fingers through the fur on Dodge's back, which was starting to rise. Dodge and Furball were not exactly friends, and right now my sister's cat was glowering in our direction. Not that Sam noticed this — she was too busy gawking at glossy photos of teen pop stars. "Who's the real teenager around here?" I asked, settling Dodge's fur. Owen might have been fifteen, but Sam was ten going on sixteen.

I stepped forward with a sigh. "Can you get your feet off the desk? It's not a footstool." She didn't respond, so I shoved her ridiculous shoes lightly to get them off the desk. "I need some —"

Sam shot to her feet, sending a hissing Furball and a stack of my favorite old mysteries to the floor. Her blue eyes flared, and she was wearing mascara, which was against the rules. "I am *so* glad I only have to share a room with you for a few more days," she snapped as she glanced down at my copy of *The Hound of the Baskervilles* before following Furball out the door.

Dodge licked my hand to let me know he was there, and I picked up the books before plopping on my bed. Part of me, a *big* part, was totally psyched that I wouldn't have to share a room with my little sister much longer. But another part was sad. Another part was already lonely. It seemed like everything was changing in my house, and all at once. Mostly it was Owen, but now it was Sam, too.

The changes started after Owen's birthday, when he announced that he was moving out of his bedroom into the bonus room in the basement. He said he "needed space." But even an idiot could see the basement room was smaller, and there was hardly any light.

Naturally, the minute Owen announced his plan, Sam called dibs on his room. I probably should have put up a fight and insisted the bigger room be mine — I'm two years older than she is. But the whole thing happened so fast. Plus I didn't want to hear one of Sam's "you have no idea how hard it is to be the youngest" rants. It's not like being in the middle is a picnic.

After that, Sam started obsessively marking the stuff she'd be taking with glitter tape. I looked around the messy room and noted that I was about to be left with my bed, a few books, and the ancient clown lamp Dad found at a thrift shop when I was three. Sam despised its faded paint and slightly torn shade, but I loved the way the night-light illuminated the clown's red nose — so much that I pretended to be afraid of the dark just so I could turn it on.

For all I knew, Sam was planning on taking the clown lamp at the last minute, out of spite. Then I'd be left with my bed, my books, and Dodge.

I felt a rush of gratitude for my dog, who had parked himself next to my bed and was looking at me with total devotion. I leaned down to push my face into the longish fur around his neck. "It'll be nice when it's just us," I said into his soft black ear. I rested my head against him for a minute, inhaling his smell — a mix of dry straw, good dirt, and cut grass. Comfort.

Dodge lifted his head and licked my face — a big beggy wet kiss. "You're right," I agreed. "We do have work to do." Grabbing the laptop Sam and I shared, I slid onto the floor next to Dodge. I did a lengthy search on Verdel Ward, reading and rereading all the recent articles about him, and started some lists in my notebook. The first included suspicious stuff: no body, no will, no friends. The second was stuff to investigate — stuff I'd need answers to: Who was the last person to see Ward? Was he really dating someone? Was there ever a —

An IM popped up on my screen.

Bittersweet: What are you doing online? Thought you finished your homework.

It was Hayley, my best human friend. Hayley had *waaay* less hair than Dodge but was just as loyal. She was also in my grade at Quest Middle, was allowed on school grounds, and never *ever* sniffed anyone inappropriately.

Clued-In: I'm working on a new case.
Bittersweet: Excellent! Murder?

(Hayley was totally into true crime.)

Clued-In: Maybe. Missing and presumed dead: Verdel Ward.
Bittersweet: The mean rich dude? Hope he stays missing! Made a new cupcake today — calling it the Elvis. Peanut butter and banana with a candied maple bacon crumble. Tell Dodge.
Clued-In: ☺

16

I told Dodge, who stopped staring at my computer screen and whimpered excitedly. "Don't worry — she'll save them for you. She doesn't even eat bacon!" I said with a laugh. "Now please stop slobbering on my shirt!" I wiped off my arm and rubbed the small drool pool that had formed on the carpet with my shoe. By the time I turned back to the screen, Hayley was offline. The girl moved fast — maybe from all that sugar.

I closed my laptop and flipped back to the first list in my notebook. "Okay, here's what we've got so far," I told Dodge, reading over the page. "The way I see it, we need to start with three things: One, who saw Ward last? Two, why is there no will? And three, does this mysterious girlfriend actually exist?"

Dodge's jaws opened in a wide, stretchy yawn. I chuckled. "It seems far-fetched to me, too. Who would want to date a greedy old grump? Maybe she was after his money and didn't know he didn't like to spend money . . ."

Or maybe she killed him, I thought. Only Mom said he disappeared swimming and the girlfriend lived far away. So that didn't make any sense. Ward wasn't the first Tempest Point swimmer to be swept out to sea. Sam was right about the caution signs, and everyone knew about the riptides. "Why would Ward swim at Tempest Point?" I had just finished writing the question when Sam barged through the door wearing sunglass-printed pajamas and holding Furball under one arm. Dodge and I ignored them, but I did close my notebook. The last thing I needed was Snoopy Sam meddling in our case. I quickly got ready for bed and snuggled under the covers. I let the questions bounce around in my head while I curled my fingers into the fur of my good dog, Dodge.

CHAPTER 3

I pulled Bunny out from under my bed. I kept him there during the day — not everyone needed to know I slept with a stuffed rabbit. Just me and Cassie. And The Sister, because we shared a den.

I circled three times and settled down. I put my head on Bunny even though Bunny wasn't a pillow. Bunny had no stuffing. I made sure of that. I made sure of that as soon as Cassie gave her to me.

I let out a slow exhale. I felt my girl's fingers in my fur. Woof. This was a favorite part of my day — the snoozy bedtime nap next to Cassie. The waiting nap while everyone in our den fell asleep. Cassie was usually first. I kept my good ear trained on her breathing. Waiting for slow and steady. The Sister took a little longer. She snored so loudly I didn't have to listen hard. The Cat was last, and tricky. She only catnapped briefly. Then she went out to hunt small creatures. Which made my escape window limited. I was up to the task, though. The Cat was not all that.

I heard a snore. Cassie's hand was slack. I waited. When The Cat was asleep I stood up slowly and leaned against the bed. Cassie's palm slipped onto the quilt. I tucked Bunny under my bed, laid a sweet-dreams lick on my girl's cheek, and was out of there.

The hallway was dark. The Mom and The Dad were awake, but the door to their den was closed. I skulked down the stairs and into the kitchen. Snout pushed the deadbolt. Paws took care of the handle. Hop back. *Swish.* *Click.* Hello, backyard. I sniffed the night air.

Night air smelled better than day air. Don't ask me why, it just did. I stood there for a moment. I sifted through the strong first smells. Got to the subtle ones underneath. Nothing unusual — at least not yet.

I crouched low, then sprang forward fast and faster. Full speed. My legs hit the grass one at a time, twice each. My back legs catapulted me off the ground. A second later my fronts were over the fence. The rest of me came along for the ride.

Thud! I landed a little harder than I liked. I didn't let it slow me down though. With a new case brewing, I needed all the sniffing time I could get. I trotted down the sidewalk at scenting pace — fast enough to make time, but slow enough to pick up anything important. It was a K-9 training skill I'd honed to perfection. I kept to the edge of the sidewalk, out of the light.

I stopped to sniff a tree, noting who had left a mark since last night. I sniffed. And sniffed. Frankie, the dachshund on Twenty-seventh, had been here for sure. He was pining for Daisy, a blonde retriever with an impressively silky tail but not a whole lot going on upstairs.

I rounded a corner and left a message on a fire hydrant. Yes, dogs used fire hydrants. But that's not all we used. The canine information network was vast. Love notes, warnings, gossip, greetings, and bits of advice were doled out on trees, signposts, fences, and tires. Like the scented warning message Lurch, a mastiff on the east side, left on the rear wheel of a rusty pickup: *Use caution around the new postal worker — he's got an itchy pepper-spray finger.* Noted.

I trotted on, inhaling information. There was a lot tonight, but nothing that would help me. Nothing case-related.

I picked up my pace, wishing that Cassie was with me. Two heads were better than one. It didn't matter that Cassie's nose barely worked. She managed to sniff out clues no matter where they were hiding. And she had thumbs. Thumbs were important.

Rounding the corner, I caught a scent that made me wag. I was coming up on the house of my good friend, Gatsby "The Nose" Gunderson. Gatsby was an old basset hound. He could barely see. But who needed good vision with a sniffer like his? Nobody, that's who. The Nose was the best in the biz.

I paused in front of the Gunderson house and let out a low bark. Muffled, so I wouldn't wake the whole family. It was all I needed. Gatsby was at the window in a flash — I saw his ears brushing against the sill.

"Bauuuuu!" He bayed back a hello before his man shushed him. Gatsby's head disappeared from the window. No Nose news. That hound couldn't be shushed when he had something to say.

I started to move on, then stopped. I cocked my ear. A door latch clicked. The back door. I slipped around the side of the house. Gatsby was waiting at the gap in the wooden fence. We wagged and put our noses together. I didn't touch noses with a lot of dogs. Not many deserved it, to tell you the truth. But The Nose was a seriously good dog. I trusted him. Almost as much as I trusted Cassie.

Gatsby could tell I was on a case. He didn't need K-9 training to be a detective. He had instinct, like Cassie. And breeding. And that nose. He snorted, huffing out air and breathing it back in small snorts. The smell of excitement was all over him. He stamped his paws. He wanted out. And in.

I considered breaking him out of his yard right then and there. A nighttime sniff with The Nose would be an unexpected bone. But my training told me it wasn't worth it. Not yet. I whimpered and wagged out a promise: I'd be back when the time was right.

CHAPTER 4

"I have a fresh pan of Death by Chocolate," Hayley crooned. The school day was over and she wanted me to come over to study. I had to admit, a batch of Hayley's homemade brownies made even algebra sound appetizing. But I had to get to Pet Rescue, where I volunteered after school and on weekends. I usually brought Dodge with me to PR, but today I'd be going alone. I wanted to put in my time and also let Gwen know I had a new case and wouldn't be as available as usual before she made up the schedule.

"Warm gooey chocolaty deliciousness," Hayley sing-songed, her hazel eyes bright. I started salivating right there on the steps. Dodge was rubbing off on me in more ways than one.

24

I let out a long sigh. "Sorry, Hay," I said, slinging on my backpack. "I owe Gwen some hours before Dodge and I really dig into the case."

"Spoken like a true detective." Hayley shrugged. "I suppose I *could* save you a brownie."

I swung my leg over my bike. Her words were music to my ears. "Would you?"

Hayley grinned. "No problemo. Now go get 'em, Sherlock."

I wheeled out of the bike rack and gave a quick wave.

The ride to Pet Rescue took about fifteen minutes, and I'd ridden the route so many times I made the turns without thinking. The low cement building was on the edge of town and had plenty of space for the animals to run around outside. I heard the *barkbarkbark*ing long before I saw PR, and smiled — the noise sounded way happier than the hungry whimperings of street dogs. Climbing off my bike, I pulled open the door and wheeled it across the cement floor to its regular space in the corner.

"Hey, Gwen," I greeted the girl behind the counter. Gwen Stroud had recently graduated from Quest High and worked reception at PR. She was amazing with the animals. "How's it going?"

"It's been pretty quiet," Gwen replied, tucking her pink-streaked hair behind an ear and standing on tiptoes to peek over the edge of the counter. She searched around my legs, then met my eyes. "Aren't you missing someone?"

She was referring to Dodge, of course. "It's sort of a long story," I admitted.

She nodded knowingly, then pointed to a paper towel bulging with pizza remnants. "I saved him my crusts."

A little lump of guilt dropped into my stomach. Dodge loved pizza crusts. Not only was I keeping my partner cooped up at home, I was depriving him of delectable snacks! "I'll deliver them with your regards," I vowed, shoving the crusts into my backpack with my cell phone. "I came right from school 'cause Dodge and I are working on a new case — the disappearance of Verdel Ward. I might need to decrease my hours for a while." I bit my lower lip. "I hope that's okay."

"Totally fine," she replied, jotting herself a note. "I just hope your mom appreciates your crime-solving skills."

I grimaced. "We're flying under the chief's radar, as usual."

Gwen gave me a serious look. "I suppose you know

best, but be careful. We don't want you getting grounded for a lifetime, or worse. You're a big help around here."

"Thanks," I said. "And don't worry — I'm always careful. Plus Dodge has my back." I picked up the pen and signed in to work as Gwen's cell phone rang.

"Now *that* I believe," she told me before taking the call.

I stashed my pack in the staff room and headed into the kennels. I did lots of different jobs at PR, but my main tasks were walking the dogs and updating their personality panels — the descriptions on kennel doors that helped match them with forever-families. I tried to be honest but positive, and thought of myself as a matchmaker. The goal was to find the right person for every dog.

As soon as I pushed open the door, the barking got louder. Most of the dogs knew me and why I was there. Excited yips filled the air and tails wagged on all sides. "I know, I know," I told them. "It's walk time." I took a couple leashes off a hook on the wall and let a new dachshund pup out of his kennel. He was small and wiggly and spotted gray — highly adoptable. He probably wouldn't be here long. Once he was leashed up, I opened a second kennel. "Hey, Brewster," I said to the large mixed breed. Brewster was older and patient — a good choice to accompany a puppy on a walk. He'd been here for several weeks and knew the drill. "Let's go, boys," I said, though the dogs didn't need any prodding. I followed them toward the back door, pausing when we got to the end of the row. A frenzied bark I didn't recognize was coming from the quarantine kennel, the small room on the end where they kept dogs that were aggressive or contagious. The room was usually empty. But not today.

"Hold on a sec," I told the dogs as I peered through the small window in the door. I could feel my brows lower in alarm as I studied the pup inside — a male rottweiler. He stood facing the wall, legs apart, barking hoarsely. Desperately. At nothing. The hair on the back of my neck rose. His behavior was bizarre, creepy, and, most of all, sad. I blinked several times before turning back to my charges and heading toward the exit.

I was watching the dogs sniff their way around the tufts of grass and fighting a sick feeling when the door opened again and Taylor Bask was dragged outside by Mace, a large black Labrador who tugged him forward so hard he almost fell over. At any other moment, it would have been funny, but I couldn't laugh. The image of the desperate dog was stuck in my head.

"I saw you looking at our latest addition," Taylor said. Like me, Taylor worked at Pet Rescue and loved, loved, loved animals. Unlike me, he was already in high school — and got paid a tiny bit for his time. "He's been doing that weird barking thing on and off since he got here — like the walls are closing in or something. Poor pup is messed *up*." He shook his head.

I nodded and swallowed hard, even though Taylor would understand the lump in my throat. You never knew what had happened to dogs before they came to PR. Humans were not always humane. "When did he get here?"

"Night before last. Gwen found him tied to the fence in front. We had a hard time getting him inside — he doesn't trust people. Can't really tell what's going on with him, but apparently he hates walls."

"Maybe I can work with him," I said. I was good with fearful dogs.

"I'm not sure you want to get involved with this one," Taylor said slowly, not looking at me. "He's completely unstable. One minute he's totally fine, and the next he's freaking out. And I mean *freaking*. I've never heard a dog lose his voice before."

I nodded. I could tell Taylor was trying to protect me. I'd gotten attached to a lot of dogs, and sometimes things didn't end well. But that didn't mean I could give up and walk away. I couldn't let a dog suffer. I had to try to help.

When the last dog was walked, I headed to the quarantine kennel. I looked through the window, took a deep breath, and opened the door s-l-o-w-l-y. "Hey there, buddy," I said in a calm voice. "I'm Cassie." I watched the rottweiler closely but didn't look directly at him — I didn't want him to feel challenged. I kept my arms low and moved slowly. Even so, he growled and feinted like he was going to bite. I watched him calmly out of the corners of my eyes as I inched along the wall. When I got close enough, I held out a relaxed hand with fingers curled in.

The dog stepped forward hesitantly, sniffed, and growled. *Well, at least he didn't bite my fist off,* I thought. I wanted to get him outside so we could have some space. Without turning my back, I reached for the catchpole — a sort of noose lead on a stick — and slipped it around his neck. He held his body stiffly. A growl stuck low in his throat, but he let me lead him out of the room, past the kennels, and out the door.

"Hard to relax in there, huh, buddy?" I asked. I was relieved to be out of the quarantine room myself — it was super stuffy. I reminded myself to talk to Gwen about moving him to a regular kennel in the back. Some of them were pretty far away from the crowded rows, so the rottweiler could have a little space without being in solitary. "I'll try to get you out of there, okay? That prison is no place for a good dog like you." We walked for several minutes while I studied him. He seemed pretty okay with the catchpole, which surprised me, and he was definitely starting to relax. After ten minutes, his hackles were practically flat.

"You're okay. You're just a huge ole puppy, aren't you, Hugo?" I named him on the spot. Hugo responded by flopping down on the dirt and starting to pant. The poor guy was exhausted!

Very carefully I leaned down and reached out to pet him. He watched my every move, but accepted my affection. I felt a tingle of excitement. Out here Hugo almost seemed like a normal dog! "You're a good dog, you know that?" I said. Hugo lifted his huge head and I scratched behind an ear. He was closing his eyes with contentment when his head jerked and his doggie Mohawk reappeared. Half a second later he was on his feet, barking ferociously.

I stepped away fast. *Weird*, I thought. There was nobody around except a woman across the street talking on her cell phone. I led Hugo in the opposite direction. "Okay, got it. No strangers. But at least you relaxed for a second, Hugo. I think there's hope for you yet."

CHAPTER 5

I stood up next to Cassie's bed and stretched. Shoulders down. Paws out. Butt up. A goooooood stretch. Then I pushed my chest forward and pressed my back legs out. One at time. To get out all the kinks. *Arroooowf.*

The air was thick with tasty goodness. Pancakes. I loved pancakes. They signaled the start of two whole days with Cassie. Plus The Dad always saved one or four for me. And pancakes came with bacon. Bacon! *Bacon!* Bacon was my favorite.

I yawned, squeaking a little on the exhale. Then I shook myself and let my ears flap. A little noise. Not as annoying as a blaring alarm, but loud enough to get Cassie to roll over. She stretched and smiled sleepily.

"Morning, Dodge." I let her rumple my fur. Most pancake mornings Cassie grabbed a book and stared at it until The Dad called that food was ready. Not today. Today she threw the covers aside and beelined it to the bathroom.

I wandered downstairs to check for accidental spills. The rest of the family shuffled to the table in pajamas. Except The Mom. She was in her running clothes. She'd been all the way to the park and back. I could tell by the smell on her shoes. Goose poop. My nose twitched and I sat down, waiting for breakfast. Then Cassie walked into the kitchen. She was fully dressed and ready to go.

After pancakes, Cassie and I were on our way. Cassie got on her bike and started pedaling. I ran alongside. I had to run fast. Not my fastest, but fast. After a few minutes I let my tongue hang out and flap back toward my ears. Not exactly dignified, but it felt good.

We raced through downtown. I barely had time to register all the smells. The chemical perfume of new store stuff. The meaty scent of the butcher. Nose-burning gas stations. Musty thrift stores. Grassy parks. Did I mention the meaty butcher? The butcher saved me turkey necks. Turkey necks were my favorite. But we passed the butcher and kept going, toward the beach. I caught a whiff of the water before we saw it. I could hear it, too — crashing waves.

Square city blocks became wide, winding roads. The houses grew. They had fences and gates. They were big. I was a little out of breath. Cassie was breathing hard, too. She checked a scrap of paper in her hand and let her bike coast to a stop. "This is it," she announced. "Seven-four-five Sea View."

We were standing outside the biggest house I'd ever seen. The front of it faced the ocean — a huge half bowl with rocks extending down to the water on either side. A rock wall circled the rest of the property. Not a tall wall. Just tall enough to say "keep out."

There were signs, too. I couldn't read signs, but I knew they told humans what to do. And what not to do. Cassie stopped in front of one to read it. But she didn't always do what she was told.

Cassie hid her bike in a bush and scrambled over the wall. I took a leap and landed next to her. "This is it, Dodge," she told me. "This is the where Ward disappeared."

I sniffed around. Ocean smells were strong, and there were a lot of them. And there was always wind. Wind swirled the smells together so you couldn't catch a trail. It blew in smells from miles away just to trick you. I caught a whiff of cinnamon rolls. Then seal. Kelp. Fish. Boat fuel. Dead jellyfish. Ham sandwich. It was so garbled I wasn't even sure The Nose could have sorted it out.

We walked away from the huge house toward the water. I bounded ahead of Cassie, hoping the smells would be clearer by the shore. On one side, huge rocks jutted out into the water, past the deep, dark waves. On the other side, a big cliff cut right into the ocean. The sides of it were almost straight. When waves crashed into it they split in half and barely slowed. I stopped on the steep trail, looking down past the big rocks to the moon of beach.

"What is it, Dodge?" Cassie asked. I wasn't sure. Something about the water made my hair stand up.

I didn't have a problem with water. On a hot day I'd take anything — lake, stream, kiddie pool. Anything. On a cool day I'd happily get my feet wet. But this water looked like it wanted to suck you down and never let go. It looked . . . hungry. I stared. I might have whined. Cassie patted me and kept going down the trail. I followed.

Fishing nets. Storm drain stink. Sea lettuce. Shellfish. My nose was still going crazy when my paws hit sand. Then the wind shifted. I felt my fur fluff the other way. New smells were blowing in. Human smells. Fried eggs and laundry soap. Somebody was close. I spun around and barked to let Cassie know.

A woman was walking fast down the trail, the only path to the beach. And she was yelling at us. "You are trespassing! Leave now or I'll call the police!"

CHAPTER 6

W ell, that only took six minutes," I grumbled as the dark-haired woman approached.

"Leave now or I'll call the police!" she shouted again.

How perfect. Most of the time it was cool having a police-chief mother. But sometimes — like right now — it was a major pain. I was exactly one phone call away from being arrested *and* grounded, and there was no way off the beach except the swirling sea or the path the woman was standing on.

I saw Dodge's lip twitch and heard a growl rumbling in his throat. I patted him gently. "I think we'd better make friends." Plastering a grin on my face, I threw up my hand in a wave. *Time to roll over and play dumb.*

I patted my pockets with my other hand, feeling for the leash I carried for emergencies. I snapped it on Dodge's collar. "Finally!" I called to the woman. "I've been chasing him for almost an hour!"

If Dodge could have winked at me, he would have. Since he couldn't, he made puppy-dog eyes, wagging and leaning into my leg like he was apologizing. "Bad dog," I told him as I smirked inside.

The woman closed in and I instantly saw the wrinkles on her forehead. She was older than my parents and didn't look like she smiled much — every line on her face pointed down. I hoped we could pull this off.

As if reading my mind, Dodge lay down and put a paw over his nose, looking ashamed.

"I'm really sorry for trespassing, ma'am. I was just try-ing to catch my dog. We'll go now, but — whoa! Is that your house?" I interrupted myself and made my eyes wide — like I only just now noticed the mansion over-looking the ocean. "That's amazing!"

The woman looked mildly amused. "Oh, no," she

replied. "I'm the housekeeper, Louisa Frederick." She held out her hand, then noticed that mine was still in Dodge's fur. She recoiled like I was elbow deep in a port-a-potty. "This is the Ward Estate."

Double bingo, I thought. Not only had we located the estate, we were in direct contact with the person who had reported Ward missing. I needed to keep Louisa Frederick talking.

"No way!" I exclaimed. "Like Ward, as in Verdel Ward? The skinny billionaire who, like, disappeared?" I did my best starstruck routine and stared at Louisa like she had keys to the kingdom. Dodge stared at her with reverence, too. And it worked.

"That's right." She nodded. "He went swimming one morning and never made it back." She pointed at the cliff side of the cove. I followed her finger to the dark, swirling water.

"You mean he went swimming *here*, at Tempest Point? Isn't the riptide super dangerous?"

"Yes, right here." Louisa confirmed. "He swam here everyday. And he knew all about the riptide." She paused dramatically. She seemed to enjoy being the center of attention, and I got the feeling she didn't have many people to talk to. "The Coast Guard warned him it wasn't safe, but my employer liked only three things: a morning swim, an afternoon cigar, and money." She practically spat the last word, and her scowl was back. "I think he liked the danger signs too — they kept other people away, kept his cove private."

"Wow," I muttered. He sounded even meaner when she put it like that. "So, how'd he drown?" Sometimes the direct route was best. "He must have known what he was doing out there if he swam here every day."

Louisa was quiet for a minute, and I wondered if I'd pushed too far. Then her eyes clouded as she gazed at the ocean. "He was swallowed," she said gravely. "One cannot trust the sea."

Her words were so matter of fact that I believed her. I looked back at the angry water and felt a shiver run up my spine. It really did look like it could eat a man. Maybe Ward had pushed his luck one time too many.

We all stared at the roiling water. Then Louisa remembered why she had come out — to run us off. "Okay. You have your dog. It's time for you to go."

"Of course," I said, smiling. "We're outta here. So sorry to take up your time, Ms. Frederick. Thanks for not calling the police." I kept babbling as I racked my brain for an excuse to linger. I wasn't ready to go — I wanted more time to explore the beach. Or better yet, the house!

I started up the path, then turned back, blocking Louisa's way. I shifted from one foot to the other, looking flustered. "Um. We're happy to leave. Only, I ran after my dog pretty far and, well, may I use your bathroom?"

Louisa eyed me. She eyed Dodge. I thought maybe she was on to us. Then she sighed. "I suppose." She walked around us and led the way up the path. "You've done me a favor, in a way — you've reminded me to set the perimeter alarm. Trespassers are the last thing I need."

CHAPTER 7

The house was big. Bigger than the Sullivans'. Bigger than the police station. Big. The laundry-soap woman led us up to the doors. She swayed when she walked. She moved slowly. Her right leg took shorter steps than the left. She used her shoulder to open the heavy door. Inside was a giant room with a hard white floor — the kind that's hard to grip.

I trotted inside behind Cassie, trying not to slip. Where she went, I went. But the lady frowned and made puffing noises. Her hair was pulled back tight. Maybe it hurt. Maybe that was what made her so mad. "Dogs aren't allowed in here," she blurted.

I looked at Cassie. I got my orders from her, not angry women with pulled hair.

Cassie brushed her off like a horse shooing a fly with its tail. "Oh, but I don't want him to run off again," she said. She walked forward, staring at the walls. The art. The big sparkly lights. I kept following. The lady just stood there blinking.

"And no one will ever know. I mean, you're the only one here, right?" Cassie's voice echoed on the hard floors.

I sat down. I tried to look polite. And small. Cassie stood beside me. I could have licked her, but didn't. "Stay," Cassie told me firmly.

I whimpered. Just a little bit, to make it seem like I was too tired to go anywhere. Her eyes told me what she really meant. Words don't always tell the truth. Eyes can't help it.

I sat. I stayed. The lady walked past me, keeping as much distance as possible. I watched her lead Cassie through a door and around a corner. I twitched my ears, keeping the good one trained on my girl. Then I got up to take a sniff around.

"This place is huge!" Cassie exclaimed from somewhere

deeper in the house. The echoes told me she was in another large room. The lady's footsteps told me they hadn't reached a bathroom. "Do you ever get lost?" Cassie asked. "Or, like, creeped out? You live here alone, right?" Cassie kept talking so I could keep tabs on their location while I explored. She was good.

I put my nose to the floor. The dominant smell was definitely old. With microwave meals underneath. Wool. Mildew. Smoke. But not just any smoke. I sniffed again. Not cigarette. Maybe wood. More than one kind? I sniffed over to a doorway off the main entry.

"Of course I'm not afraid." The lady sounded annoyed. "I'm a grown woman." The footsteps stopped. They had reached the bathroom.

I heard Cassie thank her. Then I heard a door open and click shut.

I stepped into the new room. Another big one, and darker than the entry. There were tall windows with curtains over them. There were lots of books. Old books. They smelled of dust. And mildew. I spotted a stone fireplace and trotted over to investigate. No ash piles. No wood, even. Everything was clean, including the tools.

Shiny. But the smoke smells were strong. I sniffed. Something had been burned here. Recently. I had my head in the fire box when I heard her behind me.

She was in the door, looking at me the way a hawk looks at a mouse. But I was no mouse. I stared right back. She dropped her eyes and retreated a step. I knew she didn't like dogs. But as I caught a whiff of the anxious odor coming off her — a mix of metal and cider vinegar — I discovered something else. She was *afraid* of dogs. Afraid of me. Interesting.

I ignored her and went back to sniffing. Only now the smell of fear coated everything else. I thought about growling — to send her away. But Cassie wanted to make friends. So I wagged and took a step toward her. She pressed herself against the wall.

Water rushed through the pipes in the wall. A flush. I sat. I stared. The housekeeper and I were still eyeing each other when Cassie walked in. I got up and walked back to the fireplace.

Pausing just inside the door, Cassie let out a low whistle. But she wasn't calling me. She was impressed. "This is *some* place," she said. "So how come you still live here if your boss is dead?"

"The house is still here, and I am a professional housekeeper," the woman replied briskly. "Until the estate is settled and I'm thrown out, I'm staying." Then, more quietly, she added, "It's been my home for thirty years."

Cassie nodded and started talking again. Asking questions about the stuff in the room. I tuned it out. She was buying us time. I didn't want to waste it.

I stepped back into the giant fireplace opening and gave the place a full nose scan. The tender tip of my nose brushed something small, up high in the dark. Paper. Just a scrap. Stuck to the brick. I grasped it in my teeth and was backing out when I heard a shriek.

The lady was flapping in my direction. "What is he doing? Out! Get him out of there," she shouted. "He'll get soot all over the carpet!"

Cassie called me and I went. Even though I could never get anything on the carpet. That fireplace had been scrubbed sootless.

Cassie kept up the chatter as we were shooed toward the front entry. The lady's answers got shorter and shorter. When we got to the door she practically pushed us out. Cassie kept smiling, though. She waved and said thank you.

I was ready to get out. When the door opened I practically ran. When it closed I put my muzzle in Cassie's hand.

"What's this?" She took the wet scrap of paper from me and started to look at it. "*Other*," she read. "But what's been burned off?" She got the look she gets when she's playing Scrabble. Then she glanced at the house and stuffed the scrap into her pocket. She was right. The lady could be watching.

We started down the drive, looking back once or twice. We were near the wall when the wind changed. It blew in from behind the house. And it carried a load of new smells — familiar and terrible. Chemicals. Urine. Metal. Pain.

"Let's get out of here," Cassie said. She didn't have to pull my leash. The scents on the wind made me want to run hard and fast.

CHAPTER 8

A wet nose nudged my cheek and steady blasts of dog breath warmed my face. Apparently it was time to wake up. I opened one eye and peeked at Dodge. "Morning."

The second he heard my voice, Dodge wagged and gave me a kiss. I smiled and fended him off gently. My doggie wake-up-call beat my alarm by a long shot, even on a Monday. But it didn't tell me what time it was.

I looked at the clock by my bed and groaned. "Dodge, it's six-thirty!" I could have slept another half hour — more if I'd hit snooze. Did he have to go out? Why didn't he just . . . The sound of the coffee grinder triggered my brain and I sat up. "Oh, yeah. We have work to do."

On the way to the bathroom, I felt my brain picking up speed. We hadn't made much progress since we'd gotten into Ward's house. The scrap of paper Dodge had given me had to mean something, but I had no idea what. It was just a burnt corner with a single typed word, or maybe part of a single word — since it was singed right up to the edge. It said "other." Other what? I'd been asking myself that all night. The paper was thick and rough. The kind of paper they use for certificates at school or important letters. Probably all of Ward's paper was this nice. I set the scrap down and got dressed in a rush.

With Mom moving at breakneck speed all weekend, I hadn't had a second to grill her about the case. Until now.

Dodge and I bounded downstairs to find Mom pouring coffee into a travel mug. Her bag was ready to go on the table. Another few minutes and I would have missed her. *Thanks, Dodge.*

"Hey, Mom!" I gave her a hug.

"Hey, Cas." She held her coffee out so she wouldn't slosh it while she hugged me back with her free arm. "You're awfully chipper for a Monday."

"Good weekend, I guess." I poured food in Dodge's

bowl and he wagged gratefully before burying his face in the kibble. "Barely saw *you* though." It felt kind of cruel to play the guilt card right off, but it was the only one that would keep her from rushing out the door.

Mom's face fell. I could see she felt bad, which I didn't want. But she slowed down and started talking, which I *did* want. "I know," she apologized. "I'm sorry. It's just that ever since I opened this investigation I can't get caught up. Everyone wants to talk to me, but I'm getting nowhere."

I grabbed the cereal and nodded sympathetically while I poured the milk.

"First we went round and round with the housekeeper. Useless, and she's about as charming as Ward was."

I knew that, of course.

"And Mayor Baudry has been calling. And calling. He's putting pressure on me to close the case, because as long as Ward's death is under investigation, the estate can't be settled and the city can't claim the whole thing. What Baudry doesn't seem to realize is that even if I wasn't investigating, the estate would still be in dispute. Especially with the fiancée coming to town."

Dodge's ears pricked up, and so did mine. "The fiancée is real?" I asked.

"Well, there's a real woman claiming she and Ward were going to be married. And she has a real lawyer. And a real ring. But it's only her word against a dead man's — she has no proof of the relationship."

I was about to ask what the fiancée's name was when Furball jumped onto the counter, startling Mom and reminding her that she was supposed to be on a schedule. "Oh, shoot. I was going to get in early today." She snapped the lid on her mug. "It was nice to have breakfast with you, sweetie. I'll see you tonight." She planted a kiss on my head, grabbed her bag, and was gone.

Seventh grade was pretty much like every other grade. There were things and people I liked: Hayley, science, debate, and art. And things and people I didn't like: P.E., tests, cafeteria food, and Summer.

Not summer as in swimming, corn on the cob, and lemonade. I loved that summer. Summer as in Summer Hill . . . popular, pretty, and mean to the core. *That* Summer drove me bananas — just the sight of her could make my lip curl. Which was why I did my best to pretend she didn't exist, even when I could hear her cackling and talking all the way across the entire cafeteria, closing in on the unsuspecting new girl at the table by the window.

Look away, I told myself. *This is not your problem.* Only it felt a little like it was my problem.

"Hey, have you met the new girl?" I asked Hayley. She was next to me in the lunch line, wrinkling her nose at the Tofu Surprise. It wasn't easy being a vegetarian at Harbor. I looked at the meatloaf swimming in a tray of green-flecked sauce, sealed in plastic. It wasn't easy being an omnivore, either.

"Yeah," Hayley said, curls bouncing. "Alicia, right? She's in my history class. Seems cool. Did you know she lived in Cambodia?" Hayley gave her "food" a cautious sniff before dropping it onto her tray. I left the meatloaf on the warming table and grabbed a cup of chocolate pudding and a prewrapped turkey sandwich.

I nodded that I knew. I'd met Alicia in science class and we'd spent the end of the period talking. Her parents were Civil Engineers in the Peace Corps and they'd lived all over. This was her first time in "normal" American school. Which made her a perfect target for that thing I was trying to ignore. That thing that was tossing her blonde hair, smiling, and not looking the slightest bit dangerous.

I knew from experience that, as innocent as she looked, Summer *was* dangerous. *Let it go,* I told myself. *Pretend she doesn't exist.*

But the situation was getting worse by the second. Summer and her posse, Eva and Celeste, were standing around Alicia with their matching haircuts, phony smiles, and lunches that they'd barely eat.

"Uh oh," Hayley whispered, cluing in on what I was seeing.

I felt frozen. All I could do was watch.

Alicia smiled at the girls around her, unaware that they were buzzards in disguise, there to pick the meat from her bones. She held out a hand, inviting them to sit down. Alicia thought she was making friends. But Summer was playing with her and I couldn't take it anymore.

I started toward the table.

Crossing the cafeteria was dangerous on a good day. On a bad day, it could be fatal. I dodged a yogurt spill. I stepped over a homework clutch. I was getting closer.

Soon I could hear what Summer was saying. "That's soo interesting!" she cooed condescendingly.

Alicia nodded happily at her. Then she opened her thermal eco-pak lunch container and sealed her fate.

Steam rose from her lunch, releasing the aromas of cumin, coriander, curry. . . . "Mmm," Hayley said. She was right behind me, and we were *both* stuck behind a gossiping group of sixth graders.

Alicia's lunch smelled delicious, but the exotic scent was way different than any "acceptable" lunchroom fare. It was precisely the chink in the new girl's armor that Summer needed.

Summer plugged up her nose, leading her friends to follow suit. "Ugh! What is that, BO stew?" She turned away and fanned her face. "Did you kill the goat yourself? Put a lid on that stuff before I get sick! Or maybe *you* already did." Her voice carried over the entire cafeteria, followed by a wave of laughter from her friends. Alicia's face turned red, and she cringed away from Summer's attack. My face was red, too, only I wasn't embarrassed. I was mad.

I ground my teeth together and pushed through the giggling sixth graders before Haley could stop me. I timed my stumble perfectly. With a hop and a side step I lurched, tipped my lunch, and let my cup of dark-brown chocolate pudding "slip" off my tray and land with a plop, right in Summer's golden hair.

CHAPTER 9

Everything moved in slow motion. I watched the brown glob of pudding slide down Summer's hair. I saw her expression shift from smirk to uncertainty to horror. I felt my smile threaten to split my face in two as a pudding globule dripped into Summer's eye. I heard Hayley start to laugh behind me. Every eye in the cafeteria was focused on Summer. It was beautiful. Absolutely beautiful.

But then my twenty slow seconds of bliss ended and life lurched back to full speed. The lunch aide, Ms. Croswell, swooped in. As a member of the faculty, she automatically assumed the person screaming was the one who had been wronged.

Clucking words of sympathy, Ms. Croswell led Summer away.

I tried to disappear into the crowd, hoping I had gotten away with it. But Summer would never allow that. As Croswell led her out, she pointed right at me. "Cassie Sullivan did this! On purpose!" she screeched.

Croswell turned, skewering me with her eyes. "To the principal's office, Sullivan," she barked. "Immediately!"

"Miss Sullivan." Principal Bettendorf gave me an angry look and I tried not to flinch. I knew from experience that he liked kids with backbone, which I had. And appropriate behavior, which I apparently did not. At least not all of the time.

"Pudding in the hair?" He narrowed his eyes and raised his graying eyebrows so they hovered higher than the rims of his glasses. I had to look away. Bettendorf was no dummy and he'd gotten to know me pretty well. This wasn't my first trip to his office — and probably not my last, either.

He let the silence grow uncomfortably long before asking a second question. "Are you still harboring resentment about the dog-on-campus issue, Cassandra?"

Oof. Cassandra. And of course I was harboring resentment! Summer had ruined a lot of things for me over the years, but getting Dodge banned from campus was the worst.

It had been shortly after we'd adopted Dodge. We were all a mess, especially Dodge. When Mom first brought him home, he woke up whimpering every night. I slept next to him in my sleeping bag and snuggled close whenever he started to cry. Mom said that was why we bonded like superglue.

I didn't tell my parents that Dodge was following me to school, that he would tail the bus and wait outside the school doors. After everything he'd been through, I was happy that he seemed comfortable around people again.

At first none of the school staff, including Bettendorf, objected to having Dodge on campus. Maybe it was because they knew he had police training. Maybe they just liked him. Whatever the reason, everyone overlooked the district rule banning dogs from campus.

Everyone except Summer. She tattled to her mother, who happened to be on the school board and obsessed with rules and regulations. Mrs. Hill forced the issue at the very next board meeting and got Dodge barred from school.

So Summer had basically put my dog in daily lockup.

"Maybe I'm a little resentful," I admitted, meeting Mr. Bettendorf's steady gaze. The principal looked satisfied as he nodded across the desk. "But that's not what this is about," I said before he got too gloaty. "Summer was picking on the new girl. She was teasing her in front of everyone."

Bettendorf's eyebrows arched again, and I knew he understood what I was talking about, so I went on. "She's just . . . *mean*." I swear I saw Bettendorf's smile muscles twitch when I said that. It was just a tiny movement though, and in a second his discipline mask was back.

"I will speak to Miss Hill about how to be more welcoming," he said. "But it is not up to you to punish other students. Your actions warrant consequences."

I could see it coming. I suppose I should have seen it coming *before* I dropped the pudding bomb, but Summer had weird effects on me. I was about to get detention, probably a week of it. And once my parents found out, there would be grounding, probably two weeks of it.

I clenched my fists between my knees and stared at the floor. I was about to be put in daily lockup myself and lose my investigation time for the foreseeable future.

Summer had won again.

CHAPTER 10

My toenails clicked on the kitchen floor. *Click-click-click-click. Click-click-click-click.* I was waiting and pacing. I always waited awhile after the family left. Waited before I went out. I didn't want anyone besides Cassie to know I could *get* out. They might lock me in the laundry room. Or change to round doorknobs. Round needed thumbs.

But I was ready to go out and sniff up some more clues. The creepy feeling I'd gotten at the Ward mansion was still with me. I had to find out what it was.

I walked back. *Click-click.* And forth. *Click-click.* One more time. I was about to push the handle when I heard a creak. No, not a creak. A squeak. A meow. *Oh, woof.* The Cat.

I heard the meow again. I turned and shot The Cat my mean dog look. It stopped burglars in their tracks. It had no effect on The Cat whatsoever. She just sat there on the counter. Licking some cheese.

Cheese. I loved cheese. Cheese was my favorite.

She was taunting me. I knew that. I am a smart dog. Naturally, I tried to ignore her. But *cheese.* And The Cat.

I looked. And looked. I couldn't take my eyes off of the horrible scene. And then I was on the counter. And the cheddar was all mine.

Ha! I licked my lips while The Cat hissed and scrambled to get away. Victory! "Woof!" But as soon as she was gone, I felt bad. I was too big for the counter, and I'd knocked the butter dish to the floor. I hopped down, full of shame.

I'd lost control. My ears and my tail drooped. I licked up the mess but didn't enjoy it. I told myself it was The Cat's fault. The Cat made me do it. But I knew it wasn't true. I knew I was a bad dog. I was feeling so terrible I didn't hear The Dad until he walked into the kitchen.

What? None of my pack came home for lunch. It was lucky I was still here. If The Cat hadn't taunted me I would have been gone. But I was home. My secret was safe. And I had The Cat to thank. Not that I would *ever* thank The Cat.

I wagged at The Dad and tried not to look guilty. Skulking was a dead giveaway. He didn't notice the butter dish, and the cheese was safe in my stomach. Besides, he was distracted.

"Hey, Dodger. Forgot my wallet. Got halfway to work before I remembered." The Dad scratched his head and raced around grabbing things. "Huh. Forgot this, too," he said, picking up his lunch. "Didn't even remember I forgot this. Yeesh. Where is my head?" he asked, looking at me. It appeared to be where it always was, on his shoulders. But what did I know? Then he was gone. And I was back to pacing. *Click-click-click-click.* I cocked my ear and waited for the car's engine noise to fade. I waited some more. Then I jumped up and caught the handle with my paw. I dragged it down and hopped backward on my hind legs until it was open enough to slip through. It closed on its own. I'd lost a few tail hairs in the door before, but I was getting better. With a swish and a click, I was out. I hoped The Cat was watching.

The sun hit my fur and air filled my nose. I jumped the back gate in an easy leap. I was free to do some serious sniffing! I trotted down the street and around the corner and found Gatsby in his yard. Perfect.

I put my nose to the ground, casing the Gundersons' fence until I smelled soft dirt. No clay. No rocks. I started to dig. One paw chased the other. Paw. Scrape. Paw. Scrape. Paw. Scrape. Faster and faster.

I loved digging. Sand. Lawns. Fields. Digging let out all the smells trapped in the ground. And if you did it right, it could let out your friend.

Gatsby squeezed under the fence through the tunnel I'd dug. He bayed his freedom, and I nudged him under the chin, telling him to be quiet. We were breaking out! We needed to be quiet. And fast.

Gatsby could do quiet. Fast was harder. Gatsby had short legs, and he wasn't young. It was going to take awhile to get to Ward's. But who knew what The Nose would find when we got there?

We sniffed our way into town, stopping to share a

dropped sandwich. *Mmmm.* Peanut butter. Peanut butter was my favorite. We were sniffing the town square and upsetting the squirrels when I heard a familiar voice and smelled a familiar smell. Mayor Baudry.

Mayor Baudry was not a big man. He just sounded big — all bark, like a miniature schnauzer. He smelled like onions and half-truth. He used to come to the police station a lot when I worked there. Once you smelled him, you never forgot.

We stopped by a bench to listen. The mayor was talking to a woman I'd never seen before.

"Yes, my *fee-yawn-say*." She said it in the same way The Mom told The Cat not to claw the couch. Harsh. And she held her hand like it was wounded. Or she wanted the mayor to see it. She had something. A ring. It wasn't the icy looking rings women often wore, though. It was a flat gold ring with a design.

"Verdel and I were to be may-reed in the spring," the woman said. Her voice was slow. Her hair was big. Verdel. The name she was saying was more exciting than the ring. It made my ears go up. I looked at the woman's face. I looked at her shoes. They looked good for chewing, not for running.

64

The Mayor snorted and stepped away from the woman. He probably wanted to get her perfume smell out of his nose.

"He told me ev-ah-ree-thing he had was mine, so I don't know whii we-ya fussing over a lack of will," she crooned.

"He told *me* that Bellport was the most important thing to him!" Baudry said. "And I have to ask myself why you didn't you come sooner if you and Ward were so in love?"

"Well, I . . ." The woman's eyes grew big. I could tell she wanted to nip Baudry on the flank. She blinked a bunch of times. "I was too distrah-aht!" she whined. "Besides, that ah-ful housekeeper won't let me into the house," she finished in a quiet voice.

I looked over at Gatsby to see if he'd heard that, but he had wandered off and was sniffing a trash can farther away. I whuffed, to call him back. Bad move. Gatsby didn't look up, but Baudry did, and when he saw me he showed his teeth and started making noise. Lots of it.

"Doesn't anybody enforce the leash laws in this town? What is going on here?" he yelled, huffing and flapping his arms. "Where is Animal Control?" He looked around for somebody to come after me and Gatsby. I ducked my head and hightailed it. He'd probably recognized me, but there was no way he could catch me.

Gatsby saw me rush past and ran with me. I heard Baudry still barking behind us, but nobody followed. We slowed to a trot, sniffing our way out of town. Up the road. Around a bunch of turns. Trees. Fire hydrants. I could smell the sea. Gatsby did, too. He was puffing in and out. His sniffer was on overdrive.

Finally, we got to the Ward estate. I put my front paws on top of the rock wall and surveyed the grounds. I heard a faint buzzing — the perimeter alarm was on. I gave a little woof to let The Nose know, then helped him over the wall.

I had to hand it to Gatsby. Even after our long journey he showed some hustle. I wanted to find the source of the disturbing scent. But the old basset headed straight for the beach. He sniffed up the shoreline with a vengeance, sorting the sea smells in the swirling wind. His tail flexed. His nose shivered. Then, all of a sudden, he slowed. He plodded at a snail's pace.

It had taken a long time to get here, and I was starting to worry. It was getting late. And it was a Pet Rescue day.

I wanted to get home to Cassie. "Woof!" It was time to go. The stubborn hound ignored me.

The Nose ambled forward, tail straight out. He stopped. He fixed on a small circle of paper. Special paper — the kind that doesn't shred. Gatsby pressed his nose to it. He snuffed in and out. Then he barked for me to pick it up.

I had no idea what it was. But The Nose knew. It was a clue. So I picked it up, tucking it into the side of my mouth.

Gatsby was obviously satisfied with his find, because he started up the trail toward the mansion. And thank goodness. The sun had moved pretty far across the sky — it was getting later and later. I let the ocean smells swirl past my nostrils without sorting them. I headed for the rock wall.

I was about to leap when I smelled her. Fried eggs and laundry soap. The housekeeper.

Letting out a quiet bark, I steered The Nose around the other side of the house. It would take longer to get off the property, but we had a better chance of getting away without being seen. I froze when my nose was assaulted by the terrible smell I'd whiffed the other day — the one that made me want to bolt. Only now it was stronger. A lot stronger. My hair stood up. Gatsby stopped in his tracks, too. His nose quivered. I thought he might bail. But he didn't. He sprinted straight toward a chain-link rectangle behind the mansion.

I tried to keep my cool. The smell said "run!" but I followed instead. There was no house inside the fence. It looked like a dog prison.

Before I could stop him, Gatsby sat down and let out a mournful howl. "Bauuuu!" Believe me, I wanted to chime right in. Howling was in order. But the housekeeper. I nosed The Nose, telling him to be quiet. He howled louder.

That's when the housekeeper appeared. She looked grouchier than ever — all yells and waves. I gave a sharp warning bark to get Gatsby moving, then took off toward the wall.

Thu-thump, thu-thump, thu-thump, and I was over. I landed on the other side and waited for Gatsby to appear.

But he didn't appear. He yelped.

It didn't take a detective to know that the housekeeper had him.

I hurled myself back over the wall. I curled my lips into a snarl. I charged.

The housekeeper's eyes got huge. She let go of Gatsby's collar and ran. Her slow shuffle was nowhere to be seen.

Gatsby wasted no time, either. He ran for the wall and cleared it easily. By the time I was over it, he was halfway down the block.

CHAPTER 11

I pushed open the door to Pet Rescue and almost laughed out loud. Taylor was standing in the middle of the lobby tangled in the leashes of four rambunctious pups.

"Looks like you're a little tied up," I said with a grin.

Taylor rolled his eyes. "You could say that. A little help?"

The dogs yipped as I helped them get unwound. A cocker spaniel named Jude licked my hand, either grateful or noticing the roast beef I'd had for lunch. "Here you go," I said, handing the leashes over.

Taylor gave me a goofy grin and headed out the door. I watched him go, wishing the case was as easy to unravel as the dogs' leads.

"Hey. You're here! Does that mean the case is going well?" I turned to see Gwen behind the counter, and wondered whether she'd been there the whole time watching Taylor flail or had just appeared.

"Lousy," I admitted, picking up the pen and signing in. "So far all I've got is a scrap of slobbery paper, a greedy mayor, a cranky housekeeper, and a supposed fiancée."

Gwen gave me a sympathetic look. "Sounds tough."

I nodded, feeling my forehead crinkle. "All anyone ever liked about Ward was his money. They all want it, but nobody's getting it. Why would you kill someone if you weren't *sure* you'd get the cash? I'm beginning to think there might not be a case here at all. . . ."

"Keep at it," Gwen suggested. "Something always comes up." Her eyes drifted to my legs. "Are you neglecting my favorite German shepherd?"

Sighing, I shook my head. "No, I just couldn't pick him up today. I got into a tiny bit of, um, trouble at school." I quickly explained about the chocolate pudding incident and my impending detention-plus-grounding doom.

"Wow, you *are* having a rough day. Need a sip of my latte? It's got extra whip."

71

"No, thanks." I already had a jumpy stomach. "I just came by for a little one-on-one with Hugo before my lockup starts. How's he doing?"

Gwen took a sip of her coffee and put the cup down slowly. Not a good sign. "Cassie, I'm not sure you should get your hopes up about him. He's not making a lot of progress with us." The corners of her mouth pointed straight down.

Ugh. This was the last thing I needed — more bad news. "But with me Hugo was —"

"I know," Gwen said soothingly. "Your magic was working with him. But —"

"Which shows that he's reachable." I wouldn't back down. I *couldn't* back down. "We just need a little more time."

Gwen shook her head. "You are one stubborn girl, Cassie Sullivan." She pushed a strand of pinkish hair away from her gray eyes and half smiled.

"I prefer *determined*." I lifted my eyebrows in a dare and backed away from the counter until her half smile turned into a whole grin. Then I spun and pushed through the door leading to the kennels. My palms were a little sweaty and I could feel my heart thudding. Was I nervous or upset? Probably both. If I couldn't help Hugo . . .

Don't go there, I told myself. I needed to pull it together or Hugo would smell my negative emotions like fish sitting too long in the sun. Turning, I made a last minute stop in the small staff room to give myself a minute. I shoved all my stuff into one of the lockers, took a deep breath, and pushed back into the noisy kennels.

Hugo was lying in the far corner with his chin on his front paws. "Hey, buddy, how's it going?" I called through the chain link.

Hugo lifted his head and barked roughly in response.

"I know, I know," I said. "You want to get out." I lifted a leash off the hook and slowly opened the door. Hugo got to his feet, shaking out his back legs, and took a few steps closer before stopping. I took that as an invitation to put the leash on and went for it. *Click!* Mission accomplished.

"Good boy," I told him as we walked to the back door. I wanted to avoid Taylor and his yipping pups. The fewer distractions Hugo and I had, the better. Outside, Hugo sniffed and tugged and peed in at least a dozen places.

Watching him, I felt a smile sprouting at the corners of my mouth. *Progress.*

Back inside, Hugo took a long drink and flopped down on the floor of his kennel. "Comfy?" I asked as his tongue lolled to the side. He was definitely relaxed. I leaned down and gave him a pat. "I've got to go, and I might not be back for a while. Gwen and Taylor will take good care of you, though. So give them a break, okay?" He snuffled out an exhale and actually thumped his tail. "Good boy."

Smiling, I went to get my stuff out of the locker. Finally, something was going right! I slung my backpack over my shoulder and returned to Hugo's kennel for a happy good-bye. I considered inviting Gwen in to see how well Hugo was doing.

It was a good thing I didn't.

I knew something was wrong as soon as I opened the latch. Instantly, Hugo was on his feet, hackles raised and teeth bared. The growl in his throat was menacing and directed at me. The only thing that had changed was that I was wearing my pack and not carrying a leash — nothing that seemed upsetting. Only Hugo was clearly upset.

I backed away, shocked and hurt. "Hugo?" I said quietly. "Hugo, it's me. Didn't we just have a nice walk?" His growl deepened.

With my heart in my stomach, I closed the kennel. I'd gone from victory to defeat in seconds — the story of my day.

Everything was going from bad to worse.

CHAPTER 12

The Nose and I were still on the move, making our way back home. There was no time for sniffing or lifting a leg. There was no time to rest. Not that the housekeeper was after us. I'd probably scared her enough to keep her inside for the rest of the night. I wasn't proud — I was no bully. But it had gotten messy.

Gatsby's ears dragged on the ground. His tail was low, too. He was dog-tired, and shaken. He twitched every time a car passed. Watching him, I felt terrible. I'd dragged a fellow dog into a dangerous situation. I'd compromised the investigation by letting myself be seen prowling around the Ward estate . . . twice! And I'd threatened a human.

I hadn't had a choice. I couldn't let Gatsby get dragged off. Any dog worth his license would help out a comrade.

Luckily, my tunnel under Gatsby's fence hadn't been filled in. Gatsby turned and touched his nose to mine. The message was clear: *No hard feelings. Thanks for the backup.* I whimpered in response, then barked. "Woof!" *Time to get back under that fence.*

The Nose nosed his way through, wiggling under the wooden slats. I looked through a crack and saw him amble up the stairs. He barked at the door. It opened. Gatsby was home safe.

Home. Cassie. Supper! *Supper. Supper. Supper.* I turned and ran, ignoring my aching paws. I cleared the back fence with a little effort and landed on the long grass. The Brother had some mowing to do.

Inside, The Dad was making dinner. The butter dish was on the counter. A new stick of butter was inside. I heard water running upstairs. I needed water. I took a long lap from my bowl, then trotted up the stairs. Cassie was in the shower.

I barked outside the bathroom and sat down to wait. It was the least I could do. I hadn't made it home to greet my girl . . . again! I rested my chin in my paws and closed one eye. The hall was a busy place. The Brother and The Sister were dragging boxes, bickering about who had right of way. I considered playing traffic cop, then decided against it. I let my shoulders slump and waited for Cassie. She liked long showers.

Finally, the water turned off. My tail thumped. Cassie was in there. Cassie would be out soon. I cocked my good ear. Heard her step out of the tub. Towel off. I was on my feet before she touched the door handle.

I stepped back, ready to greet her. My whole back end wagged. But when she opened the door, all I got was a feeble smile.

"Hey, boy," she greeted. "Where've you been?" Her head was low and her shoulders drooped. Her invisible tail was hanging straight down. I followed her into our room and nuzzled her hand to let her know it was all right. That I was here. She leaned her forehead into mine. I licked her cheek and remembered the clue. It was slimy and crumpled, but I gave it to her anyway.

Cassie stared at the slimy ring of paper. "What's this?" she asked, turning it over. Woof. A clue. "Thanks, Dodge." She set it on the bedside table next to the other paper scrap — the burned one — and watched The Brother carry another box of stuff down the hall.

CHAPTER 13

This is what you wanted, I told myself. *This is what you wanted, and now you're getting it.* How many times had I told my parents I wanted my own room? A thousand? A million? A lot. So why, now that Sam was leaving, did I feel so . . . abandoned?

I dropped my head into my hands. It wasn't Sam's departure that bothered me. It was Owen's.

I felt a gentle paw on my knee. Peeking through my fingers, I saw Dodge's chocolate eyes gazing at me worriedly. He was so right. I hadn't been abandoned. I wasn't alone. I had him.

I reached out and ruffled the soft spot on his head. "Why do human relationships have to be so complicated?"

Dodge licked my thumb. "I wish it were that simple," I sighed.

Owen and I used to be friends. We used to do stuff together. Then, on his fifteenth birthday, I suddenly turned into vermin. I hadn't even done anything. But just like that, everything changed.

I eyed my dismantled room. Sam had been busy, but she wasn't exactly neat. Half-packed boxes, piles of clothes, shoes, books . . . I could barely see the floor. Once Sam was gone I'd have to get Hayley to come over. She'd have this place fixed up in no time and probably bring a celebratory chocolate cake to boot. *Stop feeling sorry for yourself*, she'd tell me. *Embrace your freedom!*

I smiled in spite of myself. Hayley would find the good in this situation. And then she'd turn it into great. I looked around for my laptop — Hayley was probably online right now — but didn't see the computer. My little sister had taken that, too.

"Sam!" I shouted down the hall. "Where's the computer?"

"Duh. I'm using it," she replied snottily.

"You've had it all afternoon. My turn!"

"Patience is a virtue," she sing-songed, "that you don't have!"

I bolted to my feet, startling Dodge, and charged into the hall. Sam could be such a brat! I was going to give her an earful! I was going to . . .

Unfortunately, I was intercepted by Mom, who stood imposingly in the upstairs hall. "Were you planning on using the computer for homework, Cassandra?" she asked calmly. "Because I just got off the phone with Mr. Bettendorf, and I'm afraid you're grounded until further notice. And that means —"

"No screen time unless it's for educational purposes," I said in frustration.

"Close," she replied, arching a single brow. "Home-work only."

If I were a dog I would have howled. Loudly. But I wasn't a dog, I was a girl. A grounded, no-computer-privileges girl. Still, I had to say something. I had to try to explain. "She deserved it, Mom."

Mom bit her lip. "That may be, Cassandra, but you have to learn a little self-control. You cannot douse someone in chocolate pudding every time you don't like their behavior."

Sam let out a guffaw from the doorway of her new room. "Pudding? Who?"

"None of your business," I snapped. *Eavesdropper.*

"I'll bet I can guess. And I bet she *didn't* deserve it. I bet you were just jealou —"

"That's enough, Samantha." Mom held up a hand, and Sam made a face but kept her mouth closed. I waited for Mom to retreat after delivering my sentence, but she changed the subject instead.

"We got a call from Verdel Ward's housekeeper at the station today. She says a dog keeps coming around the Ward property. She's seen him twice now . . . a large German shepherd. And a smaller dog, too."

I forced myself not to look at Dodge. He'd obviously been busy! Maybe that was where he found the slimy ring of paper. I hadn't paid much attention when he gave it to me, but if he'd picked it up at Ward's . . .

"Cassandra?" Mom sounded impatient. "Would you care to shed some light on this?"

I shrugged, glad I really didn't know what Dodge had been up to. Lying to Mom was hard. Lying under pressure was harder. "Was it that new patrol dog, Hero? I've heard he's a little out of control . . ."

Mom crossed her arms over her chest and gave me her police chief look. "No, it wasn't Hero. Cassie, I've got enough to handle without having to take calls about a" — she cleared her throat — "wandering dog."

Dodge chose that moment to raise his chin and look up at Mom with puppy-dog innocence.

"Don't give me that look, Dodge," she said. "I know better."

I was shocked. Was Mom on to us? Suddenly revoked computer privileges seemed perfectly reasonable. Lenient, even. "Okay, got it." I said. "You won't see me near a keyboard unless it's for school."

Mom dropped her hands to her sides. "Good. Dinner is in fifteen minutes, and it's your night to set the table."

In other words: no time to look at the clue that Dodge had brought me.

Sam was on cleanup, and I cleared my plate while she whined about having to wash the enchilada pan. Halfway through my plate of tortilla, poblanos, cheese, and sauce, I'd gotten an idea.

Patting my leg, I summoned Dodge and headed to the basement. Owen had disappeared from the table early to work on his room. This was my chance to see his new setup, and hopefully get a little computer access, too. But I couldn't just waltz down the stairs. I needed an emissary . . .

"Lead the way, boy," I whispered, giving Dodge a nudge. He padded down the stairs, leaving me waiting at the top in the semidarkness.

"Hey, Dodge," Owen greeted. "Whaddya think of my new digs? Not bad, eh?" I could picture Owen holding Dodge's head between his hands and giving him a friendly shake. Dodge responded with his silly, open-mouth play growl. I waited another ten seconds, then started down.

"How's it going?" I asked, trying to sound casual. I *was* interested, of course. But I didn't need Owen to know that.

Owen got up and followed my gaze around the room. "Coming along," he said.

I looked at my brother's messy hair. At the tiny bit of

stubble on his chin. At his blank expression. He looked sort of . . . sad. And that made me sad, too.

I'd been thinking about making up some story about needing his computer, but his slumped shoulders changed my mind. "Look, I'm grounded and I need to look some stuff up online. Can I use your laptop?" I asked.

Owen frowned for a second, but Dodge leaned up against him and let out a squeaky yawn. Owen couldn't help but smile.

Nice work, I thought, watching my brother's face soften. He grappled Dodge's big head and threw a chin toward his cluttered desk. "Make it fast."

Heaving a sigh of relief, I hurried over and opened the laptop, quickly finding a homework cover page. Then I pulled out the scrap of paper Dodge had brought me and set it on the desk. It was some sort of white and gold ring, and had several letters running across it. Punching the letters in, I soon learned that the scrap was actually a custom band from a very expensive Cuban cigar. "Who would spend seventy-five dollars on one cigar?" I murmured to myself as the obvious answer popped into my head: *Verdel Ward.* Closer inspection revealed that it wasn't just pricey — it was custom. The lightning bolt design was a fancy version of Verdel Ward's initials: *V. W.* I carefully put the band back into my pocket before moving on to my next search topic — Ward's business.

Squinting at the screen, I tried to wrap my 8:00 P.M. head around what Ward did for a living. From what I could tell, wealthy people gave him their money to put into stocks or businesses or whatever he thought would make them *more* money. And according to the older investor reviews, Ward was good at it. *Amazing returns*, somebody wrote. *Out-of-the-box investment thinking, with impressive results*, said another. The most recent comments, though, told a different story. *Don't go near him*, one person wrote. *Steer clear if you value your savings*, said another. Although Ward himself was ridiculously wealthy, it looked like he'd lost huge amounts of other people's money. A few more clients reported that he didn't keep accurate records, and had stopped returning their calls.

I jotted down the screen names of a few clients who sounded most upset: SoreandPoor, DeadBroke, and MoneyHuntr. Could one of them be a suspect? It seemed possible . . .

I was lost in thought when my brother's voice butted into my headspace.

"Okay. You've had your time. Now get out."

Ouch. I logged out and closed the laptop. "Thanks a ton," I said, trying to ignore the rejected feeling ballooning in my gut. "Good night." I said it without looking at him. Then I turned and led Dodge up the stairs.

CHAPTER 14

I pulled Bunny out, circled three times, and thumped the carpet with my front paws. I lay down on my bed next to Cassie's. *Whump!* I put my head down and let out a long breath through my nose. It felt good to settle.

"I know." Cassie dropped her hand into my fur. Breathe in. Breathe out. Breathe in. Our breathing found a rhythm and we exhaled the day.

It hadn't been a good one for either of us. First Gatsby's family stapled chicken wire along the bottom of their fence. I couldn't dig through chicken wire. Not even a little. And that meant I couldn't spring Gatsby. My best canine friend was basically in jail. And it was my fault.

Then Owen closed his door. Cassie and I had to stay out. Having to stay out made my girl's ears droop. No computer. No new information about the case. No clues. No digging. No bones. We needed a bone. Dog, did we need a bone.

I closed my eyes. Cassie's fingers worked my fur, and I let them lull me. The *thump-thump-thump* of her heart echoed in my ears. Her perfect smell lingered in my nose. My mind drifted to the first night I slept by her bed. The first night I let down my guard. After. After the accident. Somehow I knew I'd found her. I didn't know I'd been looking, but I knew I'd found something that had been missing. I'd found someone I could love and trust. Just when I thought there'd never be anybody else . . .

"Dodge!" a voice called in the darkness. Was it dark? Or was I blinded by the smoke? I couldn't tell. I whimpered, confused. I couldn't see through the thick, stinging air. Couldn't smell, either. Breathe in. Breathe out. Every breath hurt. Breathe in. Cough . . .

I couldn't turn back. I had to stay. Stay. No. Had to go. Had to reach the voice. My lungs howled. I fought my way forward, toward my partner.

"Dodge! Get out!" Mark's voice choked. "Go!"

I could not go. I wheezed. I crouched lower, pulling myself on my paws. My belly scraped the floor. I squinted. Wheezed. Inched closer.

Finally, I reached him. My partner. He was lying on the floor. I grabbed his collar and tugged. He didn't budge. I pulled again. "No, Dodge. No. Bad dog! Go. Get out. Get away!!"

Bad dog? The words stung more than the smoke in my eyes. The smoke in my lungs. My chest was heavy with shame and confusion. Bad dog?

I could feel myself slipping into the nothingness. My partner went limp. Soon it would be too late. I had to get out. I had to get us both out. I braced my legs on the floor and grabbed my partner's pants in my teeth. I pulled hard. The large body shifted slightly. I felt dizzy. I braced again, lowering my body to the floor. I leaned back and pulled . . .

And a massive explosion rocked the building.

CHAPTER 15

The only good thing about detention was that I could make notes about the Ward case in peace. Leaning back in my uncomfortable chair, I reviewed what I'd written in my notebook:

1) Verdel Ward is dead.
2) Verdel Ward has no will.
3) Verdel Ward had some unhappy clients.
   a. Were any of them unhappy enough to kill him?
4) Louisa Frederick (Ward's housekeeper) was the last person to see him alive.
   a. Louisa Frederick is cranky.

    b. Is she still at the house because of loyalty, or
       does she have another motive?

5) A woman claims that she and Verdel Ward were
   engaged.

    a. Really??? Seems totally unlikely that he'd
      marry anyone, or that anyone would
      marry him!

6) Mayor Baudry wants Ward's money badly.

    a. Why doesn't he want Mom investigating?

7) Physical evidence:

    a. Burned scrap from mansion.

    b. Custom cigar band — expensive habit!

I finished reading and tapped my pencil on the table-top. *Tap, tap, tap. Tap. Tap. TAP!* Frustration fell over me like a wet blanket. How on earth could I solve this case when all I had was a bunch of questions . . . and deten-tion? I was stuck like a mouse in a glue trap. Not even reading *To Collar a Killer* was helping.

Ugh! I put my head on the table, turning my gaze to the far wall of Ms. Hahn's classroom. I stared in misery at the less-than-sparkling windows and the shelves of textbooks underneath. And then I saw them. Right there, centered in my line of sight: a small stack of newspapers.

Ms. Hahn often had her students read the paper so they could discuss current events. I looked at the stack — there could actually be something useful in there! — then at Malcolm Hitchens, the detention monitor. Malcolm was an eighth grader who looked like a forty-five-year-old man. I swear his hair was getting gray at the temples, and he often wore a bow tie to school. A bow tie! Needless to say, he took his job as detention monitor *very* seriously.

Technically speaking, you were not allowed out of your seat in detention. You were supposed to sit there and ponder your evildoings. Or something. But I didn't care about what I was supposed to be doing. I quietly broke my pencil lead.

"Can I sharpen this?" I asked sweetly. "I'll be super quick."

Malcolm adjusted his tie and eyed me suspiciously. "I suppose I can make an exception," he said. "But be aware that I am not setting a precedent." He glared at the rest of the prisoners.

I was across the room in a flash. I shoved my pencil in the sharpener and checked out the papers. The top section was sports, but I could see what looked like a front page underneath. I reached out and snatched it up. It wasn't the front page — just the finance section. My heart sank. I was about to put it back when I saw the words *For the Love of Money* printed near the top with a grainy photo of the Ward mansion underneath. Eureka! I shoved the paper under my sweatshirt just as Malcolm looked up from his *Wall Street Journal*. I hurried back to my seat.

My heart was thudding as I s-l-o-w-l-y pulled the newspaper out and spread it on my desk. I saw a tiny picture of Verdel Ward looking cranky (of course) and skeletal. He had all the money in the world but clearly didn't spend it on food. He looked like the wind could blow him over.

In contrast, there was a bigger photo of a woman who looked like a cross between Dolly Parton and a late-night news anchor. The caption below read: *Sophia Howe, alleged fiancée.* Leaning forward, I began to read.

**The estate of Verdel Ward, the late billionaire
and financier, cannot be settled until the police**

investigation led by Chief Doris Sullivan has been completed. "I have to do everything within my power to uncover any hidden truths about Ward and his death. Until we are able to do that, our work is not finished," Sullivan stated on Friday.

Meanwhile, several people are attempting to lay claim to Ward's fortune. Ms. Sophia Howe of Houston, Texas, has arrived in Bellport with her lawyer to prove that she was Ward's fiancée. "Verdel was the love of my life, and I'll do whatever it takes to prove that we shared everything," Howe tearfully declared in an interview late Friday.

Longtime housekeeper Louisa Frederick confirms that her employer made multiple trips to Texas, but claims to know nothing about a romance. "My understanding was that Ms. Howe was a business client of my employer's and nothing more," she stated. She further claimed that in the many years she worked for the millionaire she never saw or heard him speak of family or romantic associations. "He was a very solitary man."

I scanned the rest of the article. Looking at the photo, I saw Sophia Howe had a ring, but not a traditional engagement ring. She looked younger than Ward, way younger, and not exactly his type. Then again, I couldn't think of anyone who *was* his type. I wanted to talk to her. *Tap, tap, tap.* My pencil was at it again, this time with excitement. I looked at the clock. I'd be out of here in fifteen minutes and could start getting interviews and doing research . . . only, I was grounded.

I was trying to think of a way to get let off my short leash when a familiar golden glint caught my eye. Oh, no. Summer's head popped up in the window of the classroom door. When she was sure I was looking, she made a mock sad face, then covered her snotty little mouth so Malcolm wouldn't hear her cackling. I spotted Eva and Celeste behind her — all of them fresh out of volleyball practice and ready to gloat. Great. I tried to ignore them, but was strangely transfixed by Summer's fake smile bobbing in and out of the window like a freaky Barbie puppet.

My leftover banana stuck out of my backpack. It was covered in spots and looking brownish. Rotten, almost. The perfect ammunition.

You want more detention? The voice in my head asked. *A week isn't enough?* I didn't, of course. But my hand seemed to be reaching for the squashy fruit anyway. It was soft and smooth under my fingertips, and a little sticky . . .

The intercom crackled to life and the school secretary's voice filled the room. "Summer Hill to the principal's office, please," Miss Lyle said in her unmistakable South African accent. Really? Could it be true? I smirked at the shocked expression on Summer's face before her blonde head disappeared. Good riddance. Maybe she was in deep trouble. Maybe she was about to get *expelled*.

Impossible. Summer was way too calculating to get in trouble, much less big trouble. But I could dream.

I reread the newspaper article I'd found and jotted down a few more notes. By the time I was finished, so was detention . . . for the day, at least. Slinging on my backpack, I headed down the hall.

Outside the principal's office I spotted Summer gnawing a thumbnail and waiting anxiously. The rest of the volleyball team was nowhere to be seen . . . the queen had been abandoned by her court. Smiling to myself, I quickened my step and looked straight ahead toward the front doors. I was going to depart with dignity.

I was pushing down the brass door handle when I heard giggling. Summer's gaggle of followers, no doubt. I was about to shout out something rude when I recognized one of the laughs. I only knew one girl who laughed that goofily. Hayley?

Hayley! I followed the noise and found my best friend and Alicia standing around the corner, holding their stomachs. Hayley saw me coming and waved me in.

"Is she still there?" Hayley gasped. Her face was practically purple with laughter. "How'd you like my impression of Ms. Lyle?"

It took me a second to get it. Then my mouth dropped open. My hand went to my face, but I couldn't contain my giggling.

"You called Summer to the principal's office?" I choked out.

Hayley nodded. "It was Alicia's idea!"

I beamed at the two of them, full of gratitude. I knew I liked Alicia!

"Mr. Bettendorf went home an hour ago," Alicia

whispered, peering around the corner. "How long do you think she'll sit there?"

Hayley and I peeked over Alicia's shoulders. Summer was fidgeting and stewing in her own juice. It was gorgeous.

"Let's not wait around to find out." I slung an arm around each of their shoulders, feeling better than I had since the pudding incident. Not even my remaining detentions could get me down now. I had good friends, a suspect had rolled into town, and Summer was suffering, just a little bit.

Things were definitely looking up.

CHAPTER 16

The house was quiet. The coast was clear. I'd had my breakfast. My nap. I'd even avoided The Cat. But that was easy. The moment she discovered that the sun streamed through the window of her new room almost all day, she barely got up. She just lay around licking herself, the lazy beast.

I paced back and forth in front of the kitchen door. *Click-click-click-click. Click-click-click-click.* Heading out this late was risky. But I needed to do some digging. Dig up some clues. *Click-click-click-click.* Cassie was stuck at school. Couldn't do any research. *Click-click-click-click.*

"Woof!" I stopped clicking. I got going. I jumped up

and opened the door. *Swish, click!* I trotted into the yard and cleared the fence, landing on all four paws.

I moved fast on my own. I was at the mansion before I knew it. I put my paws on top of the rock wall and peered over. I had to be invisible.

No cars. That was good. No lights on, either. Also good. I leaped over the wall, landed soft and kept low, clear of the alarm that was buzzing over my head. I moved slowly, sniffing for what I hadn't found on my first visit. Or my second.

A gust of wind came up, swirling the smells. Instinct told me to take cover. To get away. Training told me there was something to find. I sniffed the walkway and the fountain out front. I lifted my leg on a hedge.

Sniff, sniff, sniff. My nose got busy as I approached the flowerbed. Asters, Hollyhock, Yarrow, plastic. Plastic? I closed in on the out-of-place odor, nosing a small electronic gadget. A remote? A tiny cell phone? I wasn't sure. I turned it over with my snout, inhaling. Plastic all right. And cigar smoke. Not unlike the tiny scrap of paper Gatsby'd found. Ward?

I picked the gadget up in my teeth, settling it between my gum and the inside of my lip. I heard something inside the house. I stifled the whuff that wanted out and crept between the flowers instead. I hopped up on my hind legs, fronts on the window sill. I had to get a look.

The lights were off. I peered into a dim hallway. A chair. A small table. A figure. A man? Yes, a man.

I held my whimper in. The man was overweight and dressed in the kind of uniform delivery men wore. He had something in his hand. I squinted. A large envelope. But delivery men usually left packages outside. They didn't go inside.

My hackles stood on end. Full extension. The man was not supposed to be there. He was bad. A bad man. He walked like he was nervous. Guilty.

The man moved down the hall and into a room. My nose twitching, I dropped and moved to the next window. I hopped up, but the curtains were closed.

I moved back to my original post. I waited. And waited. I used all of my stay. All of it. Then the man came back. He went out the door and dropped to his hands and knees. He crawled. Grown men don't do this. He crawled to the edge of the yard. He looked over his shoulder, right at me. I ducked behind some flowers.

The man was definitely not supposed to be here. The man was bad. Bad man. I couldn't let him get away.

My instincts told me to chase him. My training told me I needed backup. Get him. Get backup. Get him. Get backup. How was I going to get both?

CHAPTER 17

Hayley, Alicia, and I pushed through the doors into the sunshine, leaving Summer to stew in the hall. I kicked up some leaves and smiled at the sky.

"You guys are the best," I said, facing them. "Seriously. That was just what the doctor ordered."

"You mean what Miss Lyle ordered!" Alicia corrected with a mischievous grin.

Her hair bouncing, Hayley unzipped her backpack and extracted a rectangular Tupperware. I immediately started to salivate. Hayley + Tupperware = Yum!

"Anyone want a piece of fudge to celebrate?"

Fudge! "With nuts?" I asked, licking my lips.

Hayley nodded. "Pecans, actually."

"You're the best," I said, reaching for a piece.

"What's it taste like?" Alicia asked, crinkling her eyebrows. She peered into the container, her green eyes sparkling with curiosity. "I've never tried it."

I gaped. "What's it taste like? Chocolaty, sugary, creamy happiness, that's what."

"With pecans!" Hayley added, shaking the Tupperware slightly.

Alicia reached her slender fingers in, taking a piece. She bit into it, her eyes widening in delight. "Oh my gosh!" she said between chews.

I took my own piece and ate half, letting it melt on my tongue. Hayley's fudge was amazing. "I guess they don't have fudge in Cambodia, huh?" I said.

Alicia licked a glob of chocolate out of the corner of her mouth. "Mmm. I wouldn't know. My parents are health nuts, so sweets are off limits."

Hayley looked like she was about to cry. "No sweets?" She held the Tupperware in Alicia's direction. "Here, have another. Have three. You've got a lot of catching up to do!"

Alicia took another piece and made it disappear. I loaded up with three squares, shoving one into my mouth and the others into my jacket pocket. "I'd take more for Dodge, but he can't have chocolate."

"Right." Hayley sealed her container. "Poor Dodge."

"Who's Dodge?" Alicia asked. "And why can't he have chocolate?"

"Dodge is Cassie's better half," Hayley replied.

I was tempted to thwack her with my backpack but didn't. She had a point.

"My dog," I explained.

"And your crime-solving partner, your vacuum cleaner, your foot warmer, your best four-legged friend, and —"

Alicia's green eyes sparkled. "Crime-solving? Really? Can I get one?"

I laughed. "I'm afraid they broke the mold after he was born — he's one of a kind. Practically perfect."

"You can say that again," Hayley agreed as we walked over to the bike rack. "Except for not being able to eat chocolate. That's a major dog defect."

Alicia's phone beeped and she checked the screen. "Oh, no," she said. "I was supposed to meet my dad at home. I've got to go!" She hoisted her book bag across her shoulder and hurried up the sidewalk. "Thanks for the fudge. And the pecans! See you tomorrow!"

"I'm going to swing by the station," I told Hayley as we waved Alicia good-bye. "You want to come?"

Hayley looked excited for a second, then her face fell. "Can't. I've got a huge history project due tomorrow, and I've barely started. You're so lucky you don't have Mr. Jibs."

I nodded empathetically. "Maybe you could bribe him with some of your fudge," I suggested.

"I tried." Hayley sighed tragically. "He's diabetic."

"Ooooh, bummer." We unlocked our bikes and walked them to the corner. "I'll call you later," I said. "And hold a good thought for that project."

"Thanks," Hayley said woefully. "I'll need it."

She rode off and I swung my leg over my own bike, heading to Mom's office. I had the taste of chocolate in my mouth and my excuse for stopping by on the tip of my tongue. Luckily, I didn't need the excuse. Mom was on the phone behind a pile of papers, including the finance section from the *Gazette*, looking frazzled.

"Oh, Cassie, am I glad to see you," she said, holding her hand over the receiver. "Can you do me a huge favor and stop at the store on your way home? We need milk and eggs and —" She was cut off by the person on the other end of the phone. "I understand, Mr. Liscolm," she said into the receiver. "I'm working as fast as I can."

She searched her desk for a scrap of paper, and I picked one out of the recycling and put it on her desk, then handed her a pen.

"I'm aware of the mayor's timeline, but he's just going to have to wait. I'm not going to close an investigation prematurely just because Morris Baudry has ants in his pants."

I smirked as Mom scribbled a list of grocery items while listening to Mr. Liscolm babble into the phone. "Fine, fine. Let them assign a trustee if it makes them happy, but it won't get the money dispersed any faster. Unless there's a will, they can't begin to settle the estate until I close my investigation. When I have something else to tell you, you'll hear from me. Good-bye." She slammed down the phone.

"Walker!" she yelled to one of her officers.

Doug Walker stuck his head into my mom's office, his tall frame filling the doorway. "Yes, Chief?"

"Call the mayor's office and let them know we're not backing down on this investigation. We're going to see this through whether Baudry likes it or not."

Mom's phone beeped and her assistant's voice filled the room. "Mayor Baudry on line three," Chase told her.

Mom sighed and waved a hand in frustration. "Never mind, I'll tell him myself." She shooed me and Officer Walker out of her office and gestured for me to close the door. As soon as it clicked shut, I realized I didn't have the list. Interrupting Mom when she was on a call with the mayor was not a good idea, so I couldn't barge back in — as much as I wanted to. I'd have to wait.

Leaning against the door and trying to listen in, my eyes automatically went to the blue door in the corner — Dodge's old office. I hadn't really known Dodge back then, but I'd seen him in action plenty of times. One thing was certain: He was nothing like the shepherd who'd replaced him.

I spotted the pointed ears of Hero, the new K-9 recruit, through the window. Even from fifty feet away, I could tell he was fidgeting.

"Lay down." Hero's officer, Hank Riley's, voice was muffled through the wall.

The ears disappeared and I pictured Dodge's calm, steady face. Dodge didn't need reminders. Dodge was a pro. This new pup, Hero, had some big paw prints to fill. I felt sorry for him, in a way.

The door behind me opened, surprising me. "I've got to go," Mom said as she hurried past. "Here's the list. Thanks a million, Cassie. You're a lifesaver." She turned to Walker. "Ward mansion. Let's go."

I forced my face into a mask of boredom as I watched them rush out. A new lead for Mom was a new lead for me. And I had every intention of jumping on it.

CHAPTER 18

Once the decision was made, I was all in. *Get him.* I sprinted across the lawn, toward the man's smell. I had to reach him before he got to the gate. Before he escaped.

Get backup. I could do both. Leaping into the air, I crossed the red beam. The alarm wailed. It signaled the alarm company and the police. I'd have to give Louisa Frederick a lick for turning that on.

One down. One to go.

"Rowf! Rowf! Rowf!" I let out three big barks to let the bad man know I meant business. Sometimes my bark alone was enough to stop a perp. Sometimes I needed teeth. I bared them and surged forward.

"Rowf!" I spotted the man by the gate. He was standing up. Running away. "Rowf!" Not so fast.

He turned, saw me, and stumbled. I crouched, going low on my back legs, then leaped. Right over his hunched body. I landed and whirled to face him. I stood between the man and the gate. He had no escape.

I did my best to get a quick visual in the dim light. Not tall, not short. Heavy. Fur on his face. The smells were easy: doughnuts, wool, and cigars — could be scents he picked up from the house. But the fear . . . that was definitely coming from him.

The man staggered, then grew taller. His eyes were almost invisible in the darkness. "A dog?" he croaked.

I growled.

"Come here, pooch. I know how to deal with your type . . ."

I stood my ground. I wasn't afraid. I'd been trained to take down bad guys. I could take him down in two seconds. I waited for the right moment, then lunged. My body knocked into his. He stumbled. And then . . .

I didn't see his hand go into his pocket. I should have *heard* it, but couldn't. I only saw the Taser when it came out. I only saw it as he squeezed the trigger.

Electrodes exploded out of the gunlike weapon and hit my back, unleashing electricity and pain. Every muscle in my body seized up. I had no control. I dropped to the ground. The man stood over me while I struggled to breathe. His sneering face seemed far away.

My body twitched, jerking out of control. I couldn't move my legs. Not even when they were being pulled. When I was being dragged across the lawn. My back ached. My vision blurred. Somewhere in the distance the alarm was still wailing.

"Just the place for you," a voice said. The man? Yes, the man. The bad man.

I felt myself being shoved through an opening onto a hard surface. Concrete. There was a new pain in my back. Sharp and stinging. The electrodes were out and I could move again. *Clang!* The sound jolted my senses as I struggled to my feet. It was a door slamming. But not a regular door. A metal door. A cage door. The man had put me in the cage!

"That'll teach you not to come sniffing around here, dog," he snarled through the fence. The cage smelled awful. It made me gag. I couldn't stay in here!

My body tensed again — this time with fury. I crouched and lunged, throwing myself against the fence.

It bowed with my weight, but forced me back. I landed hard on the cold cement floor.

The man laughed. "Nice try, mutt. But I'd make myself comfortable if I were you. You're not going anywhere."

I sprinted to the edge of the prison cell, my nose against the chain link. I snarled. Foam spilled out of my mouth. The man stepped back, afraid. I could see the fear in his eyes. Smell it rising to the surface of his skin.

Then he slipped the Taser in his pocket and disappeared into the night. The bad man got away.

I barked even though I knew it was useless. I hadn't even considered a Taser. I'd trained with them, but I'd never felt one. I never wanted to again. I pawed at the concrete. I'd failed. Why hadn't I watched his hand? Why hadn't I heard it?

"No, Dodge. No. Bad dog!" Mark's voice thundered in my head, and I whimpered. I was bad. I was trapped. I was a trapped, bad dog.

CHAPTER 19

I heard the sirens coming from a long way off. They made me want to howl out the danger. They also made me want to hide. Everything was going wrong.

I'd set off the perimeter alarm to get the rest of the force on the scene. That was part of my plan. Being tasered and locked in jail wasn't. Neither was letting the bad guy get away.

The sirens quieted. Patrol cars tore into the driveway. Then came slamming doors. Voices. Smells. My head throbbed. My thoughts came slowly. I smelled hot brakes. Cold coffee. The Mom.

The Mom was here! My ears twitched. "Rowf!" I let out a short sharp bark. Then I wished I could take it back.

I had no business crying for help. Crying wouldn't help anybody. Especially Cassie.

Cassie.

I crawled to the darkest corner of the cage. I kept my mouth clamped shut so I wouldn't cry again. I remembered the look The Mom gave me outside the bathroom. She knew it was me who'd been prowling around the Ward mansion. I wasn't supposed to be here, then or now. If The Mom found out, she'd shorten Cassie's leash even more.

No crying for help. I had to get out on my own.

The sun was sinking. The lights from the patrol cars made strange shadows in front of the house. I looked at the latch on the cage. I turned my head from one side to another. It was a double latch. Made for fingers and thumbs. Fingers and thumbs working together. It would be hard to open. Maybe impossible.

I tried pushing the latch with my snout. Then my teeth. I tried paws. Snout and paws. Teeth and snout. Teeth and snout and paws. I wanted to tear the thing off. I wanted to chew it up and spit it out. I wanted to eat it. I tried, but it only tore up my mouth.

I licked my nose. It tasted like metal and blood. My blood. I closed my mouth on a whimper. There was nothing I could do with the lock. All I could do was sit. And wait.

I pictured Cassie's face. I was waiting for Cassie. *Cassie will come.*

Just sitting and waiting, I couldn't help thinking about *before*. About Mark. About Mark telling me I was bad. About Mark never coming back. Maybe Cassie wouldn't come, either. Because I was bad. I'd been spotted twice. I'd been tasered and captured. I was not a good dog anymore. *This is why they kicked me off the force*, I thought. *Because I am bad. I am not fit for duty.*

I lay down and covered my nose with a paw so I wouldn't whine. I heard a car engine. Not a patrol car, a small one. Headlights flashed over the house as it pulled into the drive. It came around the corner of the house and parked. The door opened. I smelled the person inside. Laundry soap and eggs. My hackles rose. Louisa Frederick.

CHAPTER 20

Fwap. Fwap. Fwap. Fwap. My feet slapped the pavement as I ran alongside my bike. I'd ridden over a nail right after I'd left the station and had a totally flat tire. My lungs were on fire and I had a stitch in my side, but I didn't dare slow down. I was pounding my way home so I could get a different bike and my dog. I needed both ASAP, especially Dodge. We had to get over to the Ward estate to see what Mom was on to. I had a feeling it was big.

I rounded the corner and was on Salisbury Drive — the home stretch. I thought about calling Dodge. If he heard me, he'd be out the back door and over the fence in a flash.

Gasping for breath, I dumped my bike on the lawn. I

pushed open the door and dropped down to one knee, ready for a big doggie welcome. Instead, Furball meandered by. She looked at me quizzically and dragged her tail under my nose.

"Phwuh." I blew her fuzzy tail away and rubbed my itchy nostrils. "Hi, Furb," I panted, giving her quick stroke. Furball was okay, but let's face it: A waggy-dog greeting beat a cat's aloof "hello," paws down.

I heard some noise and stumbled toward the living room, where Sam was doing homework with the TV on. That meant Dad was out and Owen was "in charge."

"Have you seen Dodge?" I asked. It was a dumb question. If Dodge were home, he'd have covered me in dog drool by now. Sam looked up, shaking her head.

"Okay," I said. "I'm going out. See you later."

I rolled Owen's bike out of the garage, ignoring the voice that told me I should ask him first. My legs were longer than they'd been the last time I'd ridden it, and my feet just reached the pedals. I sat up higher than I did on my bike, too. I pedaled as hard as I could, letting the houses slip past.

The wind picked up as I got closer to the ocean, and the temperature dropped. Shivering, I realized I was *really* hoping Dodge would be there to greet me. By the time I skidded to a stop outside the gates, I was anxious, exhausted, and chilled. Two empty patrol cars were out front, lights silently flashing. I stashed Owen's bike in a bush and crouched behind the wall to scope out the scene. The driveway was quiet, but there were lights on in a few downstairs rooms. Whatever was happening, it was happening inside.

Pulling my hoodie up over my chilly ears, I snuck over the wall. I picked the closest window and squeezed between some well-manicured shrubs. They offered little protection, and I felt pretty exposed. I looked around, half expecting Dodge to appear behind me. But the only thing at my back was the cold wind.

I peeked over the windowsill and spotted Mom inside with two other officers, Walker and Gentry, and Louisa Frederick. Gentry was wandering around, so I stayed low. Walker was taking notes, looking from Mom to Louisa and back.

Mom had her game face on. I knew the look well — she used it for investigations both on the job and at home. Louisa's lips were pinched, and her eyebrows met in the middle of her forehead. She looked offended — or maybe defensive.

I was dying to hear what they were saying and pushed gently on the window sash. The wood casing was old, but it slid smoothly. A centimeter gap was all I needed.

"You set both the perimeter *and* the house alarms?" Mom asked.

"Yes. The perimeter alarm was installed several years ago, but I've only been using it since Mr. Ward passed away."

"And the house alarm?"

"Always used."

"And you set it when you left?"

"Yes."

"But it didn't go off. And when you came back, we had responded to the perimeter alarm and found the house unlocked. And yet nothing is missing."

"That's correct."

"Do you get many trespassers? Besides dogs?"

My face flushed.

"No," Louisa admitted. I prayed she wouldn't mention the girl who'd accompanied her "runaway" dog. "We set the alarm high, so dogs and wildlife won't trigger it."

Only people, I thought. I wriggled uncomfortably.

"I suppose I was getting nervous. It's a big house and

121

I'm here alone, and now people are showing up interested in Mr. Ward's money."

Mom started to pace, and I moved into the shadows. Her flashlight bounced around the room like a laser. She was definitely looking for something, but what? She held the light on a portrait of an old guy and a hunting dog. I was confused at first, then saw what she'd noticed. It was crooked.

With her back to me, Mom crossed to the painting. She said something I couldn't make out. Louisa got up. She stepped around the big desk and took the portrait off the wall. Behind it was a metal door with an electronic keypad — a safe.

Louisa stepped in close, working the code. When she stepped back, the safe was open. She waved her hand toward the dark box carelessly. "See? Nothing here," she said without bothering to look inside. I snuffed. She'd probably cleared out the valuables when Ward went missing. After all, she had the code.

Mom flashed her light into the safe and stepped closer. When she stepped back, she held a large envelope in her hand. Louisa pulled a total fish face — mouth opening and closing with nothing coming out. Mom looked like she held Boardwalk and Park Place in a hot game of

Monopoly as she tugged some papers out of the envelope. I'd recognize that victory smile anywhere, and knew what it meant. Mom had found Ward's will.

My mind reeling, I turned my back to the wall and slid down below the window rim. Why on earth hadn't they checked the safe before? It was such an obvious place to look . . .

Unless they had looked, and it hadn't been there. Louisa knew the code and she was surprised to find a will in the safe. She had obviously looked before. Something was up.

Unfortunately, I wasn't going to be able to stick around and sleuth it out. I could hear Mom on the phone with the station. More cops would be showing up shortly, in cars, with headlights. I needed to get out of there or risk getting caught. Besides, I was getting pretty freaked about my lack of Dodge. Where was he?

I closed the window noiselessly and ran in a crouch back to the wall. Hopping over, I pulled Owen's bike from the bush. There were leaves stuck in the spokes, but I didn't bother to pull them out. I just jumped on and started pedaling. When I got far enough from the house, I turned on the headlight, grateful that Owen had one. I had to keep my eyes peeled for a big German shepherd with black ears.

CHAPTER 21

I loved sniffing — what dog didn't? But there were times when I wanted to turn my nose off. The smell in the cage was dogawful. It smelled like loneliness. And pain. And misery. Whatever had happened in this cage was bad. Very bad. I shuddered for the pup who'd endured it.

I walked from the gate to the back, to the gate, to the back. I tried to focus. I had to calm down. I had to get out.

I couldn't bark to let The Mom know I was here. But it helped a little to know she was nearby, that someone from my pack was close. And she was probably digging up something on the case. I wanted to dig up something on this case, too. That was why I'd come.

I had to calm down. I had to get out.

Cages rattled me, even when they smelled good. They made me feel trapped and exposed at the same time.

The latch on the gate had my spit and blood on it. I shoved it with my snout one more time. Ouch. Chewing metal can make a mouth hurt. And I wasn't going to get out that way. I scratched at the floor. Maybe I whined. Just once. I wasn't getting out that way, either.

Then I froze. I lifted my nose. The wind was blowing, and I smelled something good. Something great. Cassie!

I looked around. It was hard to see in the dim light. The smell was gone as fast as it had come. I opened my mouth to catch a little bit more. I closed my mouth and huffed. Cassie. I didn't smell her anymore. I thought maybe I'd imagined it. Maybe I was so desperate, I'd imagined Cassie's smell.

"Rowf! Rowf!" I barked as loud as I could. Come, Cassie! I could feel the wind taking the sound from my throat. "Rowf! Rowf! Rowf!" I barked again and again. But my girl didn't come.

I put my paws on the fence and whined. I walked to the gate, to the back, to the gate, to the back. Faster and faster.

Forget calm.

I wanted out. Out. Out. Out. I walked to the back. I looked up at the top of the fence. It was taller than the Sullivans'. Almost a medium dog taller. I pictured myself leaping the fence. I whimpered. I backed up until my hindquarters were touching the chain link.

I ran, crouched, and leaped. There wasn't room to get enough speed, but I jumped higher than I thought I could. My front paws cleared the chain link. My head was over! My chest! I was out! But I started going down too soon. My back end didn't clear.

The sharp angry fence caught my belly. It bit through the fur. It tore. I yanked my legs free and fell hard. I landed with a thud. The air flew out of me. But I was outside the fence. I was out. I was free.

I was up and running before I felt the pain. Freedom carried me. I thought it would carry me all the way to Cassie. But when I tried to clear the rock wall I missed.

Still, I was out. I could catch up. I ran through the gates. The road moved like a snake. My legs felt squishy. I ran a few more steps. I barked. Or tried to. A gurgly noise came out of my throat. That was not my bark.

I tasted blood. My blood. It came out of my throat. And then my legs stopped working. They didn't freeze, like with the Taser. They crumpled, and I crumpled with them. I could not catch up lying down. I dragged myself off the road, into the bushes. I would be fine. I just needed to rest. Just a little rest. Then I'd catch up with Cassie. I'd . . . catch . . . up.

CHAPTER 22

I searched for Dodge the whole way home, pushing my panic aside. I told myself he was working on the case somewhere. Digging up evidence. Or he was at home, waiting. Yes, he was at home.

Chucking Owen's bike on the lawn, I took the front steps in two strides. I pulled open the door, ready for some doggie drool. I got Sam's scowl instead.

"Do you know where Mom is?" She stared at me like a kid in a horror movie whose head was about to spin like a top. "There's nothing for dinner and I'm starved!"

I could tell. When Sam gets hungry, she gets mad. I stood there hoping she wouldn't attack me and tear my arm off like a drumstick. It was way past dinnertime.

Dinnertime! My jaw dropped and I reached into my pocket for the list of stuff I was supposed to pick up . . . and prepare. Not. Good.

"Uh, Mom's working late. I'm on dinner," I said in a hurry. I darted away from Sam into the kitchen. I yanked open the freezer and scanned the frosty shelves. Meatballs. A chicken. Some peas.

Next, the pantry. I found rice and canned tomatoes. And pasta? Yes! There was pasta. I dug in a basket and found a sad onion and two cloves of garlic. I got the water on for noodles and started chopping.

I clanged and banged around the kitchen, throwing dinner together. I also kept an eye on the front window for Dodge or headlights. Neither appeared.

The smell of sautéing garlic brought Owen up from his basement cave. He slouched into the kitchen and leaned against the counter. After a minute, he scanned the floor and bent over to look under the table.

"Where's Dodge?" he asked.

I stirred the noodles and tried to remain calm. "I don't know," I said, biting my lower lip.

Owen didn't say anything. He looked worried, which didn't help. Then he set the table, napkins and all, which did. A little. I hoped he'd hang out and keep me company, but he ambled back down to the basement almost right away.

I stirred frantically, trying not to cry. I was officially and totally worried about my dog. My elbow knocked a parmesan rind and it slipped off the counter. My eyes welled. There was no Dodge to appreciate the spill.

I hoisted myself up and went back to the fridge. I found a not-too-floppy head of lettuce for salad. There were a couple of cherry tomatoes on the counter, and I cut them in halves. I chopped carrots and celery. I didn't usually put celery in salad, but I needed the distraction. Plus it made it look like I'd been home longer.

Once or twice I held still and listened for a bark or a scratch.

By the time my parents came through the door I was a total wreck. "Sorry we're late," Mom said. "Mmmmm, smells good."

"Finally!" Sam whined. "I've been waiting *forever*!"

I served up five plates of spaghetti, hoping Mom wouldn't notice the menu change or ask about the shopping. Unfortunately, I had a couple of things working against me: Mom noticed everything, and Sam had a big mouth.

"Looks great, Cass. I'm starved," Dad said as he sat down.

"No. *I'm* starved," Sam said. She always had to be *more* than everyone else. More cool. More hurt. More starving. More obnoxious. I shot her a look. Bad idea. "Cassie didn't get home until seven," Sam whined. "I was so hungry I was about to order pizza. I thought she was grounded."

I kicked my little sister under the table, wishing I was wearing boots.

"Really?" Mom squinted in my direction. "You came by my office at four." Her fork dangled in midair while she did the math. "And we were going to have tacos. So you never made it to the store. Where were you?"

Um, spying on you at the Ward estate?

I glanced out the window at the dark night and realized how lonely my feet were without a big, furry head to keep them warm. "I was looking for Dodge," I said with a gulp. Tears sprang to my eyes and I hurried to wipe them away. "He wasn't here after school. I was, um, going to take him shopping. And he hasn't come home for dinner," I choked out.

"Oh," Mom said. And that was all. The room got totally quiet.

After a moment, Dad leaned over and put his arm around my shoulder. "Don't worry, Cassie. Dodge can take care of himself. He'll be back." It was true. Dodge *could* take care of himself. But who would take care of me?

For the rest of dinner I pushed my noodles around my plate. I should have been asking Mom where she went so fast. I should have been playing dumb and digging. That was what Dodge would want. But all I wanted was Dodge.

Even without my help, the conversation eventually turned to Ward. Mom explained about the supposed break-in at the mansion. "The house alarm never went off — just the perimeter — though the housekeeper claims she set it. The only prints we found were Frederick's and Ward's. And nothing was missing." She smiled a little smile. "In fact, we found something we didn't think was there." Mom chewed a noodle, savoring the suspense. "The will."

"The will?" Dad echoed.

Mom nodded with satisfaction. "The will. And it appears to be legal. But here's the weird part: Ward has left everything to his twin brother, Sebastian."

"There were two of them?" Owen asked, aghast.

"Yes. Apparently there is another Ward," Mom said. "Nobody seems to have known about him. We're trying to track him down now."

Dad stopped chewing. "Have you told the fiancée?"

Mom smiled. "No, but I'm enjoying thinking about it. It will be a pleasure to inform her that she'll be getting a fat lot of nothing. I won't mind telling Baudry that he can keep his greedy hands to himself, either. The vultures can fly back to their nests."

I stared at my plate of food. Normally a break like this would put me in a great mood. But without Dodge, I just felt numb.

CHAPTER 23

The tears started to fall just before Sam knocked on the door. "Can I sleep in here?" she asked. "It's kind of lonely in my room." She carried her sleeping bag under one arm and a pillow under the other. Not waiting for an answer, she came in and spread her sleeping bag on the floor, pretending not to notice me wiping my nose and wet cheeks. I said nothing. Furball strolled in next, curled up next to Sam, and purred.

It helped to have Sam and Furb in the room, but I still couldn't sleep. I lay awake all night, listening to their breathing. Listening for Dodge. I thought I heard scratching at the back door a hundred times. Once I even got up and went downstairs, but there was nothing. Finally the cool gray dawn light came through my window and I heard Mom head out for her run and Dad grind his coffee. Night was over.

I forced myself up and staggered down to the kitchen. Without thinking I scooped Dodge's kibble, stopped, and gulped. Dad saw and pulled me away from the dish.

"I know," he said, wrapping me in a hug. "I couldn't stop thinking about him last night, either." I let my forehead rest on his chest while my arms lay limply by my sides. I couldn't look at him. I'd break down.

"But, Cass, listen. We know Dodge. He's a survivor and he loves us. He'll be back."

When Mom came in from her run she took one look at me and held a hand to my forehead.

"I'm not sick, Mom. Just tired."

"And worried," Dad added. "She didn't sleep." They exchanged looks, and I tried to appear extra pathetic. If I played it right, I might be able to stay home . . . and look for Dodge instead of going to school.

I stayed in the kitchen while Owen and Sam ate cereal and Mom showered. When she came back, I went for it.

"I don't know if I can make it through the day." I let my head drop onto my folded arms, collapsing across the counter. "I wish I could just stay home." I peeked with one red eye to see if Mom was buying. She was.

"On one condition."

I lifted my head and waited.

"That you actually stay home. And rest." She looked straight into my face and all the way through me. She knew me too well. "I can't be worrying about your where-abouts today. I've got to attend the reading of Ward's will."

"Okay. I'll stay home." *For a while*, I added in my head as the doorbell rang.

Dodge! I went from floppy and exhausted to full speed. I raced to the door and yanked it open so fast I startled the man on the stoop — Mayor Baudry. I won-dered fleetingly why the mayor would be bringing Dodge home and pushed past him to scan the walk. Nothing. No Dodge. My shoulders slumped. Duh. The mayor wasn't there to return my dog. I suddenly felt foolish standing outside in jammie bottoms and a camp T-shirt.

"Where is your mother?" Mayor Baudry demanded. He sounded irritated. It probably hadn't improved his mood to be pushed aside by someone in fleecy PJs, but he was never smiley anyway. Not unless he was on camera. "I need to speak with her immediately," he grumped. I turned to get Mom, but she'd already appeared.

"Mayor Baudry, is this a work matter?" She had a smile on her face, but her voice made it clear that she wasn't exactly thrilled to see the mayor on her doorstep at 7:42 A.M. "You do understand that this is my home, not my office?"

I ducked back inside and stood behind Mom, silently applauding. Not everyone was gutsy enough to remind the mayor about boundaries.

"You're in uniform," the mayor replied as he shoved his way in. "That's close enough. Where can we talk?"

Mom's smile disappeared. "We can talk right here," she told him, leaving the door open and not budging from the entrance. She gave me a look that told me to go to my room, but there was no way I was leaving.

"Where's this will that's suddenly appeared? I want to see it for myself." The mayor ran his thick-fingered hand over his head, smoothing the sparse black hairs.

"You know the rules, Morris," Mom said patiently. "It hasn't been filed with the county clerk yet, so it's not a public record."

"I don't care about public record," the mayor bellowed. He puffed himself up in an effort to look Mom in the eye but didn't quite make it. "I want to see that will!"

Mom's face was steely. "Then come and see me tomorrow afternoon," she advised, "at the station." She was good.

The mayor sputtered in frustration. "Dorrie, I came to you because I thought you could help. I thought we could help *each other*."

"I'll be happy to help you tomorrow, at my office," Mom replied sweetly.

Baudry turned and stomped down the porch steps. "Just remember who you work for!" he called from halfway down the walk. It sounded like a threat.

"Oh, I do, Morris," Mom said softly. "I work for the people of Bellport." She pushed the door closed and spotted me by the coat rack. "Shouldn't you be in bed?" she asked meaningfully.

I dragged myself upstairs and flopped on my quilt, replaying the scene I'd just witnessed.

I picked up my book, but even a good mystery wasn't enough to keep me from worrying about Dodge. Time seemed to crawl, and it took all my will not to stuff my bed with clothes and climb out the window. After what seemed like a million hours, the house was finally empty. I left my phone right where it was so Mom couldn't GPS me and took off on Owen's bike.

Gatsby was waiting by the Gundersons' back gate. He liked to be outside when the sun was shining, and his Dogloo had a stash of bones to keep him busy while his people were at work. Today, though, he was going to be at work, too.

"Dodge is missing," I told him. I wasn't sure Gatsby could understand me the way Dodge did, but he looked at me with his droopy eyes and trotted out the gate when I opened it. I pulled Bunny out of my pack so Gatsby could sniff it. He went a little nuts, pushing his nose into the soft fleece and snuffing hard. "Can you find him?"

Gatsby looked at me somberly before turning and heading down the sidewalk with his nose to the ground. He was on the trail. I just hoped it was Dodge's trail and not the trail of the Kebab Kart.

"I'm going to check Pet Rescue and see if anyone's heard anything," I called as Gatsby's tail disappeared into somebody's garden. "Maybe he's headed there." I hopped on Owen's bike and pedaled. It felt good to be doing something.

I made it to PR in record time and pushed through the door. The little spark of hope glowing inside me was snuffed the moment I saw the look on Gwen's face.

Oh, no. Dodge.

"What is it?" I asked, afraid to find out.

Gwen gulped and let out a puff of air. Whatever it was, it was bad. "It's Hugo."

I must have looked a little relieved because Gwen gave me a hurt look. "They're going to put him to sleep."

I felt the wind go out of me. Hugo'd been given a death sentence! "But why? He was doing so well, and he hasn't even been here two weeks! I thought they gave dogs at least —"

"They do . . . usually," Gwen said. "But Hugo's behavior isn't settling down. One minute he's fine, then suddenly he's going ballistic. And yesterday . . . he bit me." Gwen lifted her bandaged hand. She looked apologetic.

My heart sank lower than the floor. I knew that a biting dog was a problem dog. Biting was inexcusable behavior, even at Pet Rescue.

"The worst part is that it was kind of my fault," Gwen added, dropping her eyes.

I didn't know what to say, so I just listened.

"We were doing great. I was getting him water and he even let me pet him, like you said. Then my cell rang in the office, so I ran back here to answer it. When I got back to his kennel I was still talking, so I was sure he heard me. But I must have startled him because he whirled around and . . . attacked." Gwen flinched, remembering, and let her story trail off.

My stomach lurched. "I'm going to go see him," I said. I left the lobby and walked into the kennels, but Gwen wouldn't let me go into Hugo's cage. I sat down just outside, put my hand on the bars, and wondered how this had happened.

Hugo opened his eyes. He whimpered, happy to see me, and wagged his tail. "Good dog," I told him. My voice cracked. Hugo scooted closer and looked up at me with trusting eyes. That did it. I couldn't fight them off any longer. I let the tears pour.

CHAPTER 24

I woke up slowly, struggling. I wanted to wake up. I wanted to stay asleep. I couldn't tell which I wanted more. Or which I was — asleep or awake. All I knew was that I hurt. All over. I tried to yawn and shake off the feeling, but couldn't. My mouth was tied shut with something that smelled like sock.

Panic set in. I opened my eyes wide and tried to move my legs. Moving hurt. I was on my side and couldn't see much. Then I heard voices.

"It's okay. You'll be okay." A woman. She crooned softly from behind me. I felt hands on my neck and back. Kind hands. "He's waking up."

Another voice. A man. "Okay, I have the compress

on." I didn't know what a *compress* was. The man was back by my tail. I could make out the shape of him, moving a little. He was on his knees.

I felt pressure on my belly. It made me squirm. The kind hands pushed me back to the ground and held me.

"What does it say to do next?"

When I craned my neck, I could see the woman. She took a hand away from my back and looked at her phone. "Can you see any organs?"

"Ugh! Gaw. I don't know," the man groaned.

"We're supposed to wash protruding organs with saline solution and push them back in," the woman said.

The pressure came off my belly. "There's nothing sticking out. And I don't have my contact lens solution handy," the man reported. Then the pressure was back. I think I whined.

"We should get him to the vet and call his owner."

I felt my collar being turned.

"No ID," the woman reported.

Cassie took my ID off when I was at home so it wouldn't jingle against the other license and drive me crazy. I had on only my vaccination tag. The woman leaned in close to read the small print. I could feel her warmth on the back of my neck. Then I heard other tags. Not mine, but familiar. . . .

Gatsby?

"Look, he's worried about his friend," the woman said.

Our noses touched through the sock. Gatsby's touch said it would be all right. I wanted to know what was wrong. My mouth was tied shut, but my brain wasn't working right, either. I was glad when Gatsby touched my nose again.

"Pet Rescue. Five-five-one Woodside," the woman said. "Let's take him there. If they have his vaccination records, they'll know who owns him. Besides, he could use a little rescuing."

I could?

The man counted, "One, two, three . . . lift." I felt my feet being picked up. Then pain. Nothing but pain as I was swung onto a cloth. I whined through the sock.

"Okay."

The woman's voice.

"It's okay."

Gatsby's worried eyes.

Okay. I smelled the inside of a car. Saw the roof. Heard the engine start. Then . . . nothing.

CHAPTER 25

I thought maybe I was dreaming when I heard the question. "You guys looking for a big German shepherd? Black ears, tan face?" I inhaled sharply. Yes! A big German shepherd was *exactly* what I was looking for. Only when I looked up from the counter I didn't see a German shepherd. I saw a woman with blood all over her hands and jeans.

I don't remember getting up or running toward her. "Dodge! Is he okay? Where is he?"

I either startled her, or she was already flustered. "H-he's in the car," she stammered. "We found him by the road." She followed me to the parking lot where a man was waiting by a station wagon with the hatch up. Gatsby was standing in the back, next to Dodge.

"Dodge!" I ran to the back of the car. Dodge was passed out on a bloody towel, but breathing. Gatsby bayed loudly when he saw me. "Bauuuu!"

"The little guy found him, actually," the man said. "He was barking so much we stopped to see what was going on."

I gave Gatsby a pat on the head. "Good dog." There'd be time to thank him properly later. We had to get Dodge inside.

Carrying ninety pounds of dog was not easy, even with a towel hammock and five people. Dr. Byrnes took one look at Dodge and led us to the operating room. We lifted Dodge onto the table and I cradled his head, taking off the sock they had used to tie his muzzle.

Dr. Byrnes anesthetized Dodge, and his eyes flickered as the medicine took effect. I kept petting him until the vet tech arrived and the doctor told me I should go.

"He'll be fine, Cassie. His abdomen is torn and he's lost some blood — nothing we can't fix," she assured me.

I had no desire to leave Dodge's side, but Dr. Byrnes knew what she was doing. I covered Dodge's head with kisses.

Dr. Byrnes touched my arm gently. "He's a lucky dog — lucky that couple found him when they did, and lucky to have a girl like you."

She didn't know that I was the lucky one.

I staggered back to the lobby feeling wrung out. I wanted to thank the couple who'd found Dodge, but they'd already left. Gatsby was curled up on one of the chairs in the waiting room, snoring. I stroked his long soft ears and watched him sleep. "You saved him," I whispered. "Thank you." I eased down in the seat until my neck was resting on the back.

I must have dozed off, because I woke to somebody calling my name. "Cassie? Cassie."

It was Dr. Byrnes. She was sitting next to me and looking into my face. "Dodge is fine. He's all stitched up and in recovery. I thought you'd want to know."

I blinked a couple of times and bit the inside of my cheek to make sure I wasn't dreaming. *Dodge is fine.* Dodge was fine! I threw my arms around Dr. Byrnes. "Thank you!" I squawked in her ear. That woke Gastby up and he barked, complaining and celebrating all at once.

"You're welcome," Dr. Byrnes said. "He's in a little shock and has lost a lot of blood. Another half hour on the roadside and . . ." Not even the vet could finish that thought. "Well, he's fine and that's what matters. But Cassie, I found this." She opened her hand to reveal a small electronic gadget that looked like a cross between a tiny telephone and a remote. "You really shouldn't let him play with this stuff." Her face was grave. "I know Dodge is smart, but if he swallowed this, or even parts of it, it could be very dangerous."

Of course it could! I thought. I took the thing from her and turned it over in my hands. Dodge had been known to enjoy a good chew now and again, but he wouldn't eat a phone, unless . . .

"Where'd it come from?" I asked, sitting up straighter.

"It fell out of his mouth when he was under anesthesia."

"So, where did *Dodge* get it?" I asked, looking right at Gatsby. Gatsby yawned and lay back down to finish his nap. "Gwen, did that couple tell you *where* they found Dodge?"

"Yeah," Gwen nodded. "They said he was on Sea View."

My brain started firing like mad as I put the pieces together. Dodge had gone back to the mansion, too, only somehow we'd missed each other. And Dodge had gotten hurt! *And he found this.* It had to be important. I turned the black rectangle over in my hands before tucking it into my pocket. I hoped Dodge would be able to help me figure out what it was when he woke up.

"Well, I'm glad there was *some* good news today." Gwen smiled weakly from behind the counter. "I was worried that all my pizza crusts would go to waste!"

I could tell she was trying to lighten the mood. "Dodge does make an excellent garbage disposal." Gwen half laughed. We were trying to focus on the positive, but Hugo's horrible fate still hung heavy in the air.

"I need to call my dad," I said. Everyone would want to know I'd located Dodge, and we'd need a ride home. I was halfway to the staff room before I remembered I didn't have my phone — I'd have to use the landline in the lobby. I headed back, making a quick a detour by Hugo's pen. There was still time before Dodge woke up, and not much time for Hugo.

I wasn't expecting Hugo to move, but as soon as I got close to his pen he was on his feet in a flash, snarling and baring his teeth. He looked like he wanted to rip out my throat. I backed away from the cage, breaking into a sweat. "What the heck, Hugo?"

He stared me down, his eyes slits of hatred. He was

shaking all over. Maybe Gwen was right. Maybe Hugo was crazy. But I couldn't believe any dog would be this hot-and-cold. *Something* had to be setting him off. Only . . . what?

Dodge's smell on my clothes? No. I always smelled like Dodge. Different clothes? I looked down. Nope.

Frustrated, I shoved my hands in my pockets, and instantly felt the thing Dr. Byrnes had given me — the thing Dodge had picked up near the Ward mansion. I pulled it out and stared. *That* was what was different.

I was still examining the piece of black plastic when Taylor walked in. "What's up?" he asked over the barking dogs. I didn't answer, though. I was too busy wondering if the puzzle pieces actually fit together. He peered at the little piece of plastic in my hand. "What's that?"

I flipped it over. "I don't know, but Hugo hates it." I still felt sweaty from his freak-out, but it was all making sense. Hugo's unpredictable aggression. The device. Gwen's call. Cell phones.

"I know this sounds crazy, but I think this little thingy is what's making Hugo go crazy." I waited for Taylor to laugh, but he didn't. He took out his own phone and started searching for something on the Internet.

"Not crazy," he said finally. "Look! I knew I'd read about this somewhere." He turned the screen toward me and I saw snarling pit bulls — obviously dog fighting.

"Ugh." I grimaced.

"It gets worse. Keep reading." The picture was part of an ad for a device — a remotely controlled shock device guaranteed to make your dog "attack like a champion." The fighting dogs were implanted with devices that administered shocks internally whenever their "trainers" pushed a button.

"No way." It was too awful. Awful and true. I kept reading. Below the price and description were user reviews.

This would be great, but sometimes my cell phone sets it off. I was bitten twice before I realized my phone was activating the shocker.

"Serves him right," I mumbled.

Another reviewer complained that cell phones interfered with training, that when the battery was low in the remote, it activated all the time, not just when pushed. I remembered Hugo's agitation the first day I walked him, and we saw the woman across the street on her cell.

If Hugo had the implant it would explain why he freaked when Gwen was on her phone, and why he'd turned on me when I came to say good-bye wearing my backpack with my phone in it, and just now when I'd approached him with the remote in my pocket!

"Taylor, we gotta find the chip and get it out of Hugo," I said, not bothering to hide the desperation in my voice.

Taylor nodded. "I bet we can use the chip scanner." The chip scanner located microchips implanted under a dog's skin, identifying them if they got lost.

Taylor got the scanner from one of the exam rooms and we emptied our pockets of phones and the remote. Then we went to see Hugo. He was depressed, and I was definitely a little nervous, but he didn't hold a grudge. We scanned the skin around his neck, and the little machine beeped. It didn't register an address or phone number. It just beeped.

Taylor and I exchanged looks, and I ran out of the kennel to get Dr. Byrnes.

CHAPTER 26

I heard voices in the distance and opened my eyes. The light was bright. My belly throbbed. I heard the voices again. Cassie! One of them was Cassie!

My tail thumped, but I wasn't on my regular floor. I tried to lift my head. It hurt. And my throat. There was something stuck in my throat.

"Easy, Dodge," said a voice I knew. A lab coat swam into view. The Lab Coat reached down and pulled something from my throat. A tube. It was a breathing tube. And the coat was Dr. Byrnes. Which meant I was . . .

"Easy, Dodge. I'm right here," Cassie said. She stroked my ear. It felt good. Everything else felt terrible. I nuzzled her as best I could. "Shhhh. It's okay," she said. "You're okay."

I didn't feel okay. I felt like roadkill. I lay my cheek on the floor and closed my eyes. I needed rest. But there were pictures in my head. The Ward mansion. The bad man. The plastic thing I'd found. I felt around my mouth. My tongue was heavy. Nothing. Did I lose it?

I lost it. Bad dog.

Cassie stroked my ear. "Good dog," she said, leaning in close.

Right. Good dog. I was good, not bad. I let out a long breath. I needed to rest. But suddenly my nose quivered. My hackles rose. I smelled something nasty. Something from the mansion . . .

The jail! I smelled the Ward jail! And dog. A lot of dogs, actually. And a certain one. The dog that had been captive at the mansion. He was here!

I wriggled, trying to get up. But I couldn't. "You have to stay still," Cassie told me. "You just had surgery."

Surgery? Surgery came with bandages and cones. Why did I need . . .

All of a sudden I remembered. The fence. The pain. The blood.

"We should keep him here overnight," a voice said. Gwen's face appeared over me. She touched my paw.

I didn't need to see Cassie shake her head to know she shook it. I'd have shaken mine, too, if I'd had the energy. We'd been apart for one night already. We weren't going to be apart for another. "Dodge stays with me," I heard my girl say. *Woof.* I would have barked if I could.

"Don't worry," Cassie said. "Dad will be here soon."

Not too soon, I hoped. I wasn't ready to go — I wanted to meet the other dog. The captive. I struggled. I stood. *Whoa.* Everything was moving. Spinning. I started to fall, and Cassie caught me. Some other time. I could meet the captive some other time . . .

CHAPTER 27

I tucked the sheet around the cushions on the floor and tossed a fuzzy blanket on top. Dodge watched from the couch. I knew he was grateful that I was sleeping in the living room with him. He couldn't do stairs and there was no way I'd sleep anywhere else. Last night in my room without him was pretty much the worst night of my life.

I sat on my makeshift bed, fluffed my pillow, and leaned over to give Dodge a good-night kiss. He licked my cheek.

Thump. Thump. Thump. His wet nose tickled my cheek, and I smiled as I settled under the blanket. A moment later Dodge's paw found my shoulder.

I was so tired I was sure I'd be asleep in thirty seconds, but I wasn't. I wasn't asleep in thirty minutes, either. My body was exhausted, but my brain would not turn off. Images of people swirled in my head — Sophia Howe, Ward, Mayor Baudry. I was dying to know what the will said. Did it hold the answer to this bizarre case? Or a clue? Because the pieces were not fitting together . . .

Rolling over, I pushed the case out of my head, but what came flooding in after was worse: Hugo's sad face. Even though we understood the reason for his behavior, it didn't look like he'd be rescued. I still needed to save him. But not tonight. There was nothing I could do tonight.

When the first signs of light filtered through the curtains, I got up and folded my bedding while Dodge dozed. Then I helped him get outside to pee.

"Morning sleepyheads," Mom greeted us from the table as a whoosh of chilly air blew through the open door. She was already in uniform, reviewing case notes. Luckily, in all of the excitement and drama about Dodge, she and Dad just assumed I'd gone to Pet Rescue *after* Dodge got there, not before. I didn't correct this impression, so I wasn't in any additional trouble. Plus, I think my parents just felt bad about all we'd been through.

Dodge lingered outside, sniffing around before coming back in, which I took as a good sign. Then he gobbled up his breakfast — including his meds — which I took as an even better sign. "You're already on the mend!" I told him as I poured myself a bowl of cereal.

"I'm probably going to be late tonight," Mom said when Sam came into the kitchen. "There is so much hullabaloo over Ward's will, his lawyer is going to do a public reading after it's filed at the clerk's office. I'm going to make sure things don't get out of hand, but then I'll have to catch up at the office. Can you guys handle getting dinner started?"

"Sure," I replied as my brain shifted into detective gear. "What time is the reading?"

"Twelve-thirty," Mom said with a sigh. "Let's hope it's drama free."

I spooned up my last bite and dropped my bowl into the sink before hurrying upstairs to get dressed. When I came back down, Furball was stretched out in Dodge's spot, hogging the couch. I was about to shove her off when Sam beat me to it. "Come on, Furbie. The couch belongs to Dodge today," she crooned over the cat's yowls. The two of them walked upstairs, and Dodge and I exchanged a look. Unbelievable!

"This'll be comfy," I assured Dodge, resettling him on the couch and giving him a kiss on the nose. "I'll be back right after school." Dodge whimpered and put his head down on the cushion. "I know," I said. "But it's the best I can do. And tomorrow is Saturday."

Dodge thumped his tail while I put on my jacket and pulled my backpack off the bench in the hall. "Bye!" I shouted into the kitchen, ignoring Dodge's forlorn expression — I couldn't handle having *two* sad doggy faces in my brain all day.

Outside, I hopped on my bike. I had a new tire — probably thanks to Dad. I pedaled to school, ignoring my urge to swing by Pet Rescue. It wasn't on my way, and I couldn't be late. Besides, seeing Hugo might make me feel even worse.

Hayley and Alicia were at the bike racks when I rolled in. "Hey, girl," Hayley said, checking my face and giving me a hug. I had given her the recap last night.

"Are you the welcome wagon?" I asked, cracking a feeble smile.

"Just thought you might need a little cavalry," she said.

Alicia touched my arm. "I'm so glad Dodge is —"

"Uh-oh," Hayley interrupted. "Incoming." She jerked her chin toward the drop-off circle, where Summer was climbing out of her car. My friends flanked me and we headed toward the main doors.

"I think we're clear," Alicia whispered with a giggle, but too soon.

Summer was on our heels in a second. "Where were you yesterday?" she sneered.

"Pet Rescue," I told her.

"Were you getting your shots, or just visiting your cousins?"

I turned and glared, wishing my brain wasn't too drained to come up with a clever retort.

Alicia paused and turned. "She was getting inoculated against rabid seventh graders who get called to the office and stay there for *hours*, even when the principal isn't there," she said without missing a beat.

Summer's mouth dropped open, her cheeks turning bright red.

I hid my face behind my hand and cheered silently.

Hayley stifled a laugh and yanked open the door, nearly knocking Summer off the top step.

I was smiling my thanks at both of them when the bell rang. "See you at lunch," Alicia said with a wave.

I waved back and followed Hayley upstairs before saying good-bye. "Thanks for meeting me."

Hayley nodded and dug around in her messenger bag. "No problem," she said, thrusting a tiny takeout container into my hand. "For sustenance," she explained. "You look pretty wiped."

"Thanks," I said. "See you in a few." I slipped through the door and into my seat, ignoring Summer's glare from across the room. Ugh. On top of algebra, a case that felt like an unraveling sweater, and my worries about two dogs, I had to deal with her, too.

By the time lunch rolled around, I was a grumpy bundle of nerves. I set my mostly empty tray on the table and slumped into my seat. I hadn't even touched the treat Hayley had given me before first period. In fact, I'd forgotten all about it.

"Didn't you even try it?" Hayley looked offended. She reached my backpack and pulled out the little box on top. It was slightly squashed.

"This is the thanks I get for getting up at six o'clock to make your favorite toffee bars?"

Alicia eyed the box longingly. "Toffee bars?"

Hayley handed her the box. "You can have them," she said. "Cassie has clearly lost her appetite . . . and her mind."

Alicia hurriedly finished her hummus and cucumber sandwich on whole grain, then opened the tiny container. "Ooooh," she said, pulling out a bar. "This looks amazing." She took a bite and chewed blissfully. "And it has pecans!"

"Thank you, Alicia," Hayley said ceremoniously. "I'm glad *someone* still has her appetite and taste buds intact." She looked steadily across the table in my direction, her dark eyes clouded. "Cassie, everything is going to be fine. Gwen and Taylor will do everything they can to save Hugo."

Alicia licked the chocolate off her fingers. "Who's Hugo?"

As I filled her in, Alicia's face went from curious to sad to horrified. "That's awful," she breathed. Her eyes glistened. The new girl wasn't just funny, she was tender. "I had a dog when we lived in Somalia. Gusto. I cried for two weeks when we had to leave him behind. He moved in with another Peace Corps family, but I still wish I'd snuck him out in my suitcase. I really miss him."

I blinked and sat up straighter — the idea of sneaking out triggered something. My mind started to churn — and a plan started to form. I needed to get close to the case again. And that meant sneaking myself somewhere I shouldn't be.

CHAPTER 28

I pedaled down the sidewalk away from school. Fast.

I checked my watch. 12:22. I had exactly eight minutes to enact my plan, no Dodge, and I was skipping school. I tried not to think about the lecture I'd get from my parents if they found out. The courthouse loomed ahead, on the corner of Second. I swung a leg over the seat as I rolled to a stop in front of the bike rack. Next to the curb stood a fancy silver car with a license plate that said HUNT-R. Something about it pricked at my brain, but it didn't connect to anything.

Pulling my hood over my head, I walked into the building and tried to look as invisible as possible. I had one small problem: I didn't know where the clerk's office was. My best guess was one of the upper floors. I glanced at the crowd in front of the elevator and pushed gently through the door to the stairwell. My heart was pounding from fatigue and nerves when I cracked open the door and peered into the wide, pillared hall on the fourth floor. It was empty.

I tiptoed to the first door and peeked through the little window, but the glass was thick and I couldn't see a thing. I opened the door and saw a desk and sign that read COUNTY CLERK. Right spot, but nobody was around. They must have been doing the reading somewhere else.

I moved on to the next door and knew that this room was occupied. I could hear murmurings and see dark shapes around a table through the thick textured glass.

I took a deep breath and opened the door a crack. ". . . Executor of Verdel Ward's estate." Yes! I'd found it. There were some low built-in bookshelves between me and the heavy oak table, and everyone's back was to the door except for the man reading. He had to be the clerk, or a lawyer, because he had the undivided attention of his audience. Mayor Baudry, Sophia Howe, and Louisa Frederick were leaning in and listening to the man's every word as if their lives depended on it. My mother watched them intently. They were all so absorbed, I decided to risk going in. I crouched and pushed the door open just enough to fit through, then closed it silently behind me. Staying low, I half crawled around the corner and took cover behind the bookshelf as the man continued to read.

". . . do hereby give all of my tangible property and all proceeds of insurance to my twin brother, Sebastian Ward," the man behind the table read.

There was a sharp intake of breath in the room.

"I protest! I have ne-vah even heard of this bru-thah!" Sophia whined.

"Well, I had never heard of *you*!" Louisa piped up. The women glared at each other.

"This will is invalid!" the mayor blasted, getting into it. "If there's a brother, where is he? What if he doesn't show up? Does it mention anyone else? I vote it goes to the city!"

"That's ridiculous," Louisa Frederick could not hold her tongue. "This is not up for a vote!" She shot to her feet looking grumpier than ever, despite her white blouse and the colorful scarf tied around her neck. "I managed the Ward household for thirty years. I can certainly manage the estate if Mr. Ward's brother can't be located."

Sophia flapped her hand in Louisa's direction. "Yo-wah, the maid," she scoffed.

Louisa's eyes flashed. "Housekeeper," she corrected. "Besides which —"

"Besides which" — a man's voice interrupted authoritatively — "none of this is actually necessary. Verdel Ward's twin brother has been located."

My head swiveled. How had I not heard the large man come into the room? He practically filled the entire door frame. He had gray hair, and if he looked down and to the left, he'd be staring right at me! I scrambled around the edge of the bookshelf, knocking my knee. Mom's head turned. I swear her hearing was better than Dodge's!

My heart thudding, I wrapped my arms around my knees and tried to make myself as narrow as the shelf. Mom would be furious if she knew I was here!

"And you are?" Mom asked.

"Sebastian Ward, of course," the man stated, huffing his way forward.

There was a collective gasp, and I had to put my hand over my mouth so I wouldn't utter one of my own. Verdel Ward's twin was here!

I peeked around the shelf at the man, gaping. This was Verdel's brother? Except for his sparse salt-and-pepper hair, he looked nothing like the photos of the scrawny millionaire I'd seen. He was . . . fat!

For a long moment the only sound in the room was the man's heavy footsteps on the marble floor. Everyone stared, openmouthed, as he approached the table waving some sort of document. A birth certificate? Part of the will?

I was so busy gawking that I forgot to hide. I didn't see Mom walking toward me until she was standing over me, glaring. I braced, waiting for her to let loose. Instead, she leaned toward the shelf like she was looking for a book.

"That's the end of the show for you, young lady," she said, speaking so quietly I could barely hear her. "I suggest you depart as discreetly as you arrived, and make your way back to school. We will discuss this later."

What? No public humiliation? I could see the tiredness in her eyes, and suddenly realized how embarrassing it would be if my presence were known. I hadn't thought about that. She turned and walked back toward the group, while I, feeling like an insect, crawled to the door and saw myself out.

CHAPTER 29

Cassie was coming. I eased off the warm couch, stretching gingerly. I shook out my legs. I was one sore dog.

The key slipped into the lock. I wagged. "Woof." Finally! The door opened and my girl dropped to her knees. Oooh, yes! I welcomed my scratch around the ears. Heaven! I took a minute to lap up the love, then stood meaningfully by the door. I was ready to go out. I had work to do. I wasn't 100%, but wanted to be back on the job.

"Hold on, I need to get a snack," Cassie told me. She disappeared. I heard another key in the lock. "Woof." What now?

I stepped back and The Mom appeared. "Hello, Dodge. I see you're feeling better." She smelled stressed but reached out a hand. "Cassandra?"

Uh, oh. Cassandra was never good. Cassandra was Cassie's trouble name. Cassie slunk into the hall. If her ears were big enough to be useful they would have been flat against her head. She looked *and* smelled stressed. And guilty.

The Mom was all over her. With words. "You could have gotten me into a lot of trouble today, Cassandra Sullivan," she said. Only not with her usual strength. Or Chiefiness. She was dog-tired. I knew how she felt.

Cassie dropped her head. "I know. I'm sorry. I don't know what came over me. I just —"

The Mom halted her with a "stay" hand, and Cassie sat down. She had her commands mixed up. "I'm not going to punish you, because I know you've been through a lot in the past few days. But if I catch you sneaking out of school and spying ever again there will be *significant* consequences."

Cassie looked like she'd been caught drinking out of the toilet. "I understand," she said.

"Good. Now I've got to get back to the station — I just came by to pick up Ward's bank records." The Mom walked into the kitchen and grabbed a fat envelope, then pulled a yogurt from the fridge. "Ironic, really," she said to herself as she shoved the yogurt and a spoon into her bag. "I wonder if everyone would be so fired up about Ward's money if they knew how little he had left."

If Cassie had shepherd ears, they would have been standing straight up. She followed The Mom into the kitchen.

The Mom picked up an apple and took a bite. "He was paying out huge sums of money to a foreign account every month. At the rate he was going, he'd have been broke by the end of next year."

I half listened while I paced in front of the door. Money didn't make much sense to me. I knew it was a motive, though. I was ready to motivate. I paced. *Click-click-click-click*. Patiently. *Click-click-click-click*.

Didn't The Mom just say she was leaving? Shouldn't she go? Now? Cassie and I had work to do!

Let's go, let's go, let's go, I told Cassie with my eyes.

I stopped pacing and began to pant. I panted. And panted. I drooled on the floor — just a small puddle. Tiny, really. *Let's go, let's go, let's go*. I whimpered — just a little. To remind her.

171

At last she looked down. That was better. But then her gaze went back up to The Mom. Down to me. Up to The Mom. Down to me. "Mom. I think Dodge has to go."

Finally. Cassie smiled. She still smelled nervous. Like she was planning to do something she wasn't supposed to.

"I'm going to take him for a walk."

I wagged. Yes! *Woof!* A walk.

The Mom gave us a long look. "Okay, but on leash," she said slowly. "I don't want him pulling out his stitches."

Cassie cringed. We hated the leash. Didn't need it. Didn't want it. But I *was* recovering. And if that was what it took to get out of here, I'd do it. I trotted into the laundry room and pulled the dangling end of the leash off the washing machine. Cassie snapped it onto my collar and opened the door. I tugged her gently forward. Okay, maybe not *gently*. But not forcefully, either.

Cassie yanked me back. *Oof!* She never did that. "Sorry, boy. No running."

Fine. No running. We walked. To the sidewalk. Up the block. Toward Gatsby's. It was hard to go slow. I sniffed my way up to his fence. He was there, at the gap. I put my nose right up to his. Saying thank you. *Thank you for saving me.* Gatsby wagged. Then he let out a l-o-n-g "bauuuuuuu."

I raised my head. "Whuff! Woof!" Yes. I was fine. I was back on the job.

Gatsby bayed again. Mournful. He let it turn into a howl. "Bauuuuuuuu." He wanted to come. But the chicken wire under the fence said "no."

Cassie tugged. "Time to go, Dodge." She sounded impatient but was pulling in the wrong direction. I stood there, confused. Where was she going?

"Dodge, come."

It took me a minute, but I sniffed out her plan. She was going to Pet Rescue, to get the captive. Good idea. He'd know the best way in.

CHAPTER 30

I wrinkled my nose and checked my watch. Our hiding place — behind the Pet Rescue Dumpster — wasn't exactly glamorous. It was perfectly positioned, however, and spacious — there was plenty of room for both of us.

PR would be closing in two minutes. The animal center closed early on Friday so the staff could get a little break before the busy weekend.

The back door opened and Dr. Byrnes stepped out. Dodge wriggled. "You can thank her later," I promised quietly. "Right now we're laying low."

I could feel the whimper trapped in his throat, but he stayed still. I kissed his neck. The sun was setting and I leaned closer to his warmth. "You're lucky you have a fur coat," I whispered as we got back to watching the door.

After what seemed like forever, Gwen emerged slinging her messenger bag over her narrow shoulder. She punched in the code for the alarm system and climbed onto her scooter. Turning the key, she revved the engine a little and sped away. I waited patiently, listening to the sound of the motor fading. When I couldn't hear it, I looked to Dodge. His good ear was cocked — he was still listening. Even with only one good ear, Dodge's hearing was a zillion times better than any human's.

"All clear." I straightened, stretching my achy legs, and worriedly wondered how Dodge was doing. I hadn't checked his stitches since this morning. "You okay?"

Dodge trotted over to the patchy grass and lifted a leg, balancing perfectly. "Well all right, then," I said, heading toward the door. I punched in the code and the lock slid open. We were in.

I wiped my palms on my jeans and stepped inside. This was breaking and entering. Well, not exactly. I did have the code. And I was an employee. But it wasn't as if I could do what I was about to do when Pet Rescue was open. It wasn't as if I had *permission* . . .

The dogs went nuts when they heard and smelled me, barking and jumping. It was a little overwhelming in the dim light. I couldn't see well, but had to stick with the power-save lights. We did *not* need to light up the place like a beacon.

Hugo was in quarantine and barking like mad. But he was barking and *wagging*. I opened the kennel and he bounded up to me, licking my face. I felt my pocket — cell phone present. Hugo and Dodge gave each other a good, long sniff, making a nose-to-tail doggie yin yang. "Hugo, Dodge. Dodge, Hugo." I introduced them while they introduced themselves. Circle. Sniff. Wag. There was a lot of wag. Hugo was free of his control device and could finally be himself — a big, friendly guy.

I snapped a leash on him and we walked back past the kennels. "Sorry, everyone," I told the pups. "No walks until tomorrow." Ignoring my nerves, I led Hugo and Dodge outside. My fingers trembled as I punched in the code. Gwen and Taylor would definitely suspect I was the dognapper if they found out, but by then I'd have proof that Hugo was a good boy — that he could live with a family. We just had to foster him to prove it.

We walked up the empty street to the intersection that marked the border between the warehouse district and the edge of downtown. I was looking forward to getting my dog duo home and settling in for the night. Maybe everything would work out okay, even. Then, out of the blue, Dodge pulled hard on my arm.

"Dodge, come on! We've got to get Hugo home," I said, looking over my shoulder. "He's contraband."

Dodge whimpered, pulling harder. I was surprised by his strength so soon after his surgery. His back legs seemed rooted to the sidewalk. "Rowf!" His bark was sharp and insistent.

"*Shhhh!*" I scolded. But Dodge wouldn't stop pulling. Whatever he wanted, he wanted it badly. I could see there was no use arguing with him. "Okay, fine." I let him take the lead and he pulled me down the street. "Whatever your plan is, I hope it's good."

Dodge didn't answer — he just kept moving. Hugo bounded along behind him, loving the exercise. It was all I could do to keep up. By the time we got to the edge of town, the sun was sinking, the wind was picking up, and I understood. We were going to Ward's.

No sooner did I realize where we were headed than Hugo slowed down. Waaayyy down. When the mansion came into view, he stopped altogether.

Dodge pulled.

Hugo whimpered.

Dodge pulled.

Hugo sat on his haunches.

I was about to be split in two!

"Dodge, hold on!"

I turned to Hugo. "I'm not totally clear on the plan, either," I admitted. "And I get that you don't like it. But I'm pretty sure we need you to come with us. Do you think you could do that, Hugo? Please?"

Hugo cocked his head, letting out a bark. "Aroof!" Then he stood up and walked s-l-o-w-l-y. "You know this place, huh?" I asked. Then I realized: Of course he did! Wasn't this where Dodge found the remote? *Duh!* Hugo was Verdel Ward's dog!

Anger came on the heels of revelation. "That nasty old dude was zapping you, wasn't he?" I asked, pausing to give poor Hugo a hug. Some people were just plain *mean*.

Dodge pulled. "We're coming!" I called as I gave Hugo a final encouraging pet.

We made our way to the wall and I helped Dodge over. If his stitches hurt, he didn't show it. Hugo, on the other hand, was not shy about his reluctance. Getting *him* over the wall required several forceful shoves. I started to scramble over behind them when Dodge let out a *whuff.* He stared at me meaningfully. I stopped. Then I got low.

"Right. The perimeter alarm." I whispered. I rolled over the wall and dropped. We made our way across the lawn like a SWAT team.

We were right in the middle when I heard a familiar *bauuu.* Gatsby! We stopped for a second and the basset caught up, sides heaving and tongue lolling.

"Nice going," I congratulated The Nose as he and Dodge greeted each other. Gatsby gave Hugo a sniff and a wag, and it was back to business.

"This is quite the dream team," I whispered as the dew seeped into my jeans. Talk about backup! Still, I was nervous. I didn't even know the plan!

"Now what?" I whispered to Dodge. He lowered his head and led us around to a kennel. This was where Ward locked Hugo up. We huddled together at a distance, staring in the moonlight at Hugo's cage. No wonder he hated kennels. Ears flattened, and the mood was somber. "No place for a dog," I agreed.

Dodge let out a sad whimper, and we circled back toward the dark mansion. Dodge sniffed his way along a hedge by the back door, looking for a way in. Gatsby followed. Hugo, though, was shaking. I put a hand on him. He was dropping hair, too — being here was obviously super stressful. If he hadn't been on a leash, he definitely would have bolted.

Dodge came over and nuzzled Hugo, whimpering and licking his face. A pep talk.

It worked. Hugo moved in front of me and tugged on the leash, leading us to a small door under a kitchen window. It looked like a giant doggie door and was big enough for a twelve-year-old girl to squeeze through. Nice!

I pushed. It gave, and we all went through. We were greeted by total darkness. Where were we? I fiddled with my pocket and pulled out my phone.

Whoa! We were standing together at the top of a short, steep staircase. Two more steps forward and I would have fallen! "Let's go, boys," I said as Dodge started down. We scrambled after him in the near darkness. At the bottom of the staircase was a storage room with a clay floor and cases of something that looked like wine. Hugo crossed the space in my beam of dim light and started up another set of stairs. It ended at a second door. I turned the handle and pulled. *Creeeaaak.* The dogs walked through, the tags on their collars clanking. The hairs on the back of my neck rose as I propped the door open and lifted my cell phone into the air.

We were in the kitchen. I saw a big old stove, a wooden table, and cabinets that ran all the way to the ceiling. I was totally out of breath, as if I'd been running a marathon. My heart beat wildly.

This was definitely breaking and entering — my second infraction in one night! If my parents knew where I was, I'd be totally, completely busted.

They don't, I told myself. I squinted in the dark while the dogs sniffed around. Whether they were looking for a snack or clues I wasn't sure. Then Dodge froze. A barely audible growl escaped his throat. I considered turning on a light — being able to see would be nice. But before I could reach for the switch, I heard a clatter in the next room.

All four of us froze. Silence. Then we heard footsteps coming toward us, and a low, menacing, "Who's there?"

CHAPTER 31

Grrrrr. I stood perfectly still for three seconds. Long enough to figure out where the footsteps were coming from. To catch a whiff. I'd smelled this guy before . . .

Hugo yelped, and I saw the leash jerk.

"Ow!" Cassie cried. She dropped the lead and Hugo bolted down the stairs. I sprinted after him. Cassie and The Nose heeled.

I took the stairs four at a time, ignoring my stitches. We burst out the little door and sprinted toward the sea. After Hugo. I knew we wouldn't catch him. Knew how fast a scared dog could run. But we had to get out of there.

Gatsby made good time for an old hound. We raced down the trail to the beach, then stopped. Stood. Panting on the dark sand. Listening. We listened until we were sure we weren't being followed.

I wanted to run back and bite the guy. He deserved a bite. A bone crusher. But Cassie was upset about Hugo — I could smell it. I could feel it, too.

"Some rescuer I am," she said. She was mad at herself. And sad.

I licked her hand. It was okay. We'd find him. Somehow we'd find him.

We sat on the sand, huddled in the dark wind. My stitches felt tight. Achy. We were one dog down. Stranded. Upset. Going back past the house was too risky. We had to wait it out. I stared at the swirling water. I still had the smell of the man in my nose. Stuck, like a foxtail.

What did The Mom say? Something about Ward. He'd never leave his money. He was greedy. Greed had a smell. It smelled like tuna and axle grease and onions. *Woof.* Ward wouldn't leave his money. Couldn't leave it.

Maybe he didn't.

CHAPTER 32

I sat on the sand with Dodge and Gatsby, wishing I could bury myself in it. I'd lost Hugo, jeopardized the case, and was stranded with two dogs — one injured and one ancient — on a cold, dark beach.

Some detective I turned out to be. At the moment I felt more like a criminal.

I was starting to wallow when Dodge sat down, leaning into my leg. I had Gatsby on the other side. I wasn't alone. There was that. The lights hadn't come on in the house, and I didn't hear any sirens. So we appeared to be safe — for the moment. There was that, too.

We sat for a good long time. Gatsby rested. Dodge stared at the sea. I worried about Hugo. After awhile Gatsby got up and sniffed out a trail on the sand. I had no idea what he was looking for, but at least one of us was looking.

Next to me, Dodge watched the water like a statue. "What are you staring at?" I asked, stroking his soft ears. "It's the same ocean it's always been."

Gatsby ambled up and nosed my hand. I opened my palm and he dropped something into it. "Eww, Gatsby!" I said, feeling cold slime. I held my phone up and saw that it was a cigar butt. Gross. Dodge leaned in and took a sniff, then whimpered. Before I knew what was happening, he was off like a shot, sprinting toward the water.

"Dodge?" I called, expecting him to stop at the shore. He didn't even slow down.

"Dodge!" He dove into the crashing waves. I leapt to my feet and chased after him, plunging knee deep into the freezing ocean. "Dodge, no!"

I could barely see his figure in the moonlight, moving steadily away from the beach. He ducked a wave and came up again.

"Dodge!" I screamed.

I had no idea if he could hear me, but knew it didn't matter. He wasn't listening. My heart in my throat, I watched him swim farther and farther, picking up speed.

And then, all of a sudden, he was caught in the riptide and moving faster than a dog could swim. A lot faster. He was swept out, away from me, beyond the breakers. A moment later he disappeared in the black water.

"D-ah-ah-dge!" I screamed. I couldn't see him at all anymore — wasn't even sure where he'd just been.

"Bauuu-auuu-auu," Gatsby bayed, leading the way up the path. I followed, and we scrambled out to the cliff that jutted over Ward's cove. Cold water sloshed in my shoes. Below us, waves crashed against the rocky wall with alarming force. I could feel the tears coming. I didn't care who saw us anymore. Dodge was out there!

"Bauuu-auuu-auu," Gatsby bayed again anxiously. The moon cast a faint reflection on the ocean, but the churning water twisted the light. I couldn't see a thing. I shivered and realized that Dodge must be half frozen. If he wasn't already under. Oh, God. Dodge.

He needed help. I needed help. We needed help.

I pulled out my phone and stared at the time. 9:59. I hesitated, wondering who to call. My parents would kill me. I was supposed to be on a short walk, not a dognapping, breaking-and-entering escapade!

I looked at the screen for a long time. Finally, I dialed.

CHAPTER 33

My legs ached. My lungs burned. My stitches throbbed. My nose was useless. Filled with water. I was dog-tired. How much farther? There was no way to know. There was nothing to do but keep going. Keep going.

A wave crashed over my head. I sucked water up my snout. It burned. I sputtered. My legs stopped. Just for a second. A second was all it took. I started to sink. I jerked my head up. Above water. I had to stay above water.

Cold. I was so cold. I forced my legs to move. My eyes stung. I pumped. And felt it. The sucking ocean was letting go. Not pulling. Not hungry. I swam sideways then. Away from the hungry current. Along the beach. The next beach. The safe beach.

Only I couldn't get there. Couldn't get out. I told my legs to move, but they didn't listen. Bad legs. Move. The waves lapped at me. I thought if Ward couldn't leave it, he could make it. But maybe he couldn't make it. Maybe I couldn't make it. Maybe nobody could.

A wave crashed over my head. Maybe I was going to drown. . . .

CHAPTER 34

My heart leapt with joy when my brother's head appeared in the moonlight. "Owen!" I shouted, running. I threw my arms around him, and he squeezed me in a tight hug. Owen peered down at me, his hands on my shoulders, and I felt like he was holding me up.

"Okay. What's going on? Give it to me straight."

"Dodge is out there! He swam out to sea!"

"Whoa, whoa," Owen said as he took two flashlights out of his backpack. "Can you back up a little?"

I took a deep breath and explained in a rush about Ward. And Hugo. And the case. And the breakout. And the break-in. Owen took it all in, nodding.

"If he swam out there, we need to search the shore," he said, handing me one of the lights.

I nodded and wiped my cheek with my sleeve. "Are you cold? You look cold." He pulled a fleece out of his pack. "Put this on. We don't need two of you with hypothermia."

Dodge . . . hypothermia. I put on the cozy jacket.

"If he was washed . . . I mean, if he swam back to shore, he'd be east of the cliff." Owen gestured with his hands, and I pretended not to hear the "washed ashore" part. That wouldn't be Dodge. That *couldn't* be Dodge.

Owen led the way down the other side of the jutting rock wall. Gatsby insisted on coming with us, and did an impressive job keeping up on his short legs.

"Spread out, but make sure you can see my light," Owen said when we got to the bottom. I was glad he was giving orders. Glad somebody had a plan. I numbly searched the shoreline, searching for a familiar shape. For Dodge. I clamped my mouth shut so I wouldn't start to sob. Dodge . . .

"Bauuuu." Gatsby's echoing bark rose in the air, and I turned. Dodge! My beam of light searched the beach, but I didn't see the basset. He bayed and bayed, like he'd treed a fox.

"Bauuu-auuu-auu!"

Where was he?

I raced toward the sound, struggling in the soft sand. I couldn't see him!

Then my beam settled on a dark opening in the rock face — a cave. I raced toward it and ducked inside just in front of Owen. I held my breath, shining my light frantically in all directions. Sand, rocks, a puddle, and . . .

"Dodge!" I dropped down next to him, putting a hand on his side. He lay limp, his fur sopping and stiff with salt. He was exhausted, but alive. I leaned in and kissed his cheek, and he let out whimpery breath. "Oh, Dodge," I said. I crouched over him and we breathed together, forehead to forehead.

Owen kneeled beside me, checking his stitches. "They look loose, but they're intact. I think the cold saltwater might have been good for them." He gently stroked Dodge's flank.

Gatsby started to bay again. "Bauuu-auuu-auu. Bauuu-auuu-auu." Over and over.

"Good boy, Gatsby," I said, looking up. "You found him! Twice!"

But the hound wasn't looking at Dodge. He wasn't even looking in our direction. He was digging up something in the corner of the cave.

"Whatcha got, boy?" Owen asked. His light flashed on the spray of sand piling up behind Gatsby. "What is that?"

Owen got to his feet and crossed the cave. "Whoa," he said. "Check this out." He tugged on something dark sticking out of the sand, and it grew and grew, like a scarf being pulled out of a hat. When it was finally free, I blinked in surprise.

Owen was holding a man's wetsuit.

CHAPTER 35

I could barely move. I just lay there. I lay there trying not to notice the cold. My throbbing belly. Trying to take it easy. To focus on Cassie. Cassie came like she always did. Good Cassie.

I licked her face weakly. It was all I could do. The swim had almost done me in. Almost finished me. I'd basically given up when my feet touched the bottom. I staggered out. My fur was a mess. My eyes burned. Everything looked hazy. But I'd survived the swim. The ocean had not swallowed me. And it had not swallowed Ward, either.

The ocean hadn't washed away the greedy smell. The greedy smell was still in my nose. I'd followed it to the cave. The greedy smell filled the cave. I tried to bark when

I got there. Only I fell down instead. I fell down and lay there until Gatsby showed up. He smelled it, too. And he barked for me. The Nose knew. Hugo knew.

Verdel Ward could still be alive. *Was* still alive. He was the man in the house, the man Hugo was running from, the man who tasered me. The man who smelled like tuna, onion, axle grease, and smoke. It still hung on his wetsuit.

I could see The Brother holding up the suit, shining his flashlight over it. The light reflected off a tiny metallic circle with a zigzag design. A lightning bolt.

I raised my head just enough to nuzzle Cassie's arm. To let her know. Cassie pointed to the bolt. She opened her hand. She had the cigar. Gatsby's cigar. And the paper circle. The same sign.

"Check this out — a perfect match. Ward lives." Cassie showed The Brother. "Isn't this the same lightning initial symbol that was on the Halloween candy? It's a *V* and a *W*. Verdel Ward."

"So . . . this suit is Ward's? You think he swam away?" The Brother lifted the suit. "You think he's alive?"

"Of course I am," sneered a voice from the cave entrance. "You don't think I'd let someone take all of *my* money, do you?"

I raised my head, growling. It was him. Tuna. Grease. Onion. Smoke. Ward.

"Verdel Ward?" Cassie inquired.

"Mr. Ward?" called a new voice. Female. My nose quivered. Laundry soap. Fried eggs. Louisa Frederick.

Louisa stepped into the cave behind Ward. "Is that you? Why, you're . . ."

"Fat," The Brother said.

"Thanks, punk." Ward pulled the Taser out of his pocket. I heard it this time. I growled. But I couldn't get up. "Can't look too identical to my 'twin,' now can I?" He aimed the electroshock weapon at The Brother. He pulled the trigger.

"I di —" The Brother slumped onto the sand. I knew the pain and helplessness he felt. How it felt to be frozen.

Cassie screamed.

My legs finally obeyed. I was on my feet. Snarling. I felt weak, but I stood my ground. I barked, and it sounded pathetic.

Ward laughed. He released the Taser. The Brother groaned and rolled over. Ward aimed at me.

Cassie stepped between us. "You're done torturing animals."

Ward laughed. I tried to move between him and Cassie. Too late. He pulled the trigger. My girl fell right into me. We were both on the ground.

"That's enough, Verdel!" Louisa shouted. She rushed forward and kicked him behind the knees. Knees are soft. He fell forward, heavy on the cold sand.

The Brother rolled. He grabbed the Taser and aimed it at Ward. He rubbed the spot where the Taser darts had gone into his chest. "This is for you," he said. "A little thank you for those Halloween mints." He squeezed.

CHAPTER 36

I set the pizza box on the floor and flipped open the lid. Two slices of cheese — full slices, not just crust. "Here you go, boy," I told him, petting his soft-again fur. It had taken a good hot bath, an entire bottle of conditioner, and over an hour of combing, but Dodge's coat was finally back to normal. And he smelled good, too!

"Woof!" Dodge barked and leaned in, getting a noseful of extra cheese before inhaling it.

"Somebody's hungry," Mom said with a smile.

"Save room for my sweet potato cupcakes!" Hayley said, waving a brown paper bag in the air.

"He deserves every bite of both." Owen held out a plate with a piece of my favorite — sausage, pepper, and mushroom — and I almost fell over. My brother was serving *me*? He shrugged, hiding a smile and ducking past Mom, who was moving in.

"Yes, he deserves it, and so do you, Cassie. I can't thank you two enough."

I took a big bite. "Thanks, Mom. But it was really Dodge. He proved that the swim was possible — that Ward could be alive. After that, everything just came together."

"Don't forget Gatsby." Owen said, rubbing the basset's ears.

The Gundersons were so happy to have him back after he joined our investigation, they'd agreed to let him to come over for the after-party . . . or anytime.

I tossed Gatsby a crust, since a full cheese slice might keep the little guy up all night. Not that he didn't deserve a pie to himself. He did and then some. Gatsby gobbled up the goods.

I stretched a piece of melted cheese until it broke and swirled it around my finger. "Dodge, you owe your little buddy big time," I said with a smile, sitting back to enjoy my slice.

"It's still hard to believe that Verdel Ward faked his own death." Dad sounded a little offended. "But at least that explains why there was no body . . ."

"Dad!" Sam protested. "Stop talking about dead bodies!"

"He's definitely alive!" Mom and I said together. Though it was hard to believe.

"And how about that Sophia Howe? Money Hunt-R indeed. I knew I didn't like that woman the moment I met her — and not just because of her big hair." Mom was a practical hairdo person all the way.

"Do you think that's why Ward tried to swindle her? Her giant Texas hair?" Hayley asked.

"I think Ward tried to swindle *everyone*," I said flatly. "The man was a crook."

"*Is* a crook!" Owen corrected. He nudged me with his shoulder and very nearly smiled.

"Not anymore. His illegal doings days are over," Mom pronounced. "When Sophia Howe found out he was siphoning money from his clients, she blackmailed him. But she was as greedy as he was and kept raising the stakes. When Ward realized his fortune would soon be gone, he needed a way to disappear *and* keep his cash. The answer was right outside his front door — Tempest Point. 'Drowning' in that riptide seemed like the perfect plan. And since he swam there daily, he was already training for it. I had no idea Sebastian was really Verdel when he showed up at the reading of the will."

"It was a clever disguise," Dad agreed. "A beard. Forty or so pounds. But Cassie and Dodge could smell the truth."

"So true." Mom toasted us with her pizza. "I thought we'd find one criminal, but we ended up finding three. Ward is looking at extortion, corruption, and fraud. Sophia Howe is facing blackmail charges. And Louisa Frederick is charged with obstruction of justice for burning the original will."

Mom held up the scrap of scorched paper Dodge had pulled from the fireplace a week before. I'd totally written it off, but it explained why Louisa was so surprised to see the will in the safe after the "break-in," and why the house alarm hadn't gone off that night. Ward knew the code, which made it easy for him to turn off the alarm, enter his home, and place a new copy of the will in the safe, where it was was soon discovered.

"So, she burned the will?" Sam asked. "Why?"

Mom put down her pizza. "There are only two reasons to scrub someone's toilets for thirty years: love or money. Nobody loved Ward. Louisa's not an evil person, just an angry one. She saw she wasn't in the will and wanted her due, so she acted like there never was one. And if she hadn't burned the will . . . and Dodge hadn't jumped in the ocean . . . and Gatsby hadn't dug up the wetsuit . . . and Hugo hadn't ID'd the guy . . ."

I knew Mom was saying thank you, that she was proud. But hearing Hugo's name made me flinch. I pushed my plate away. Solving a case felt great. But losing a dog felt awful. Hugo may have escaped death row, but life on the streets was a sentence in itself. The poor pup would never know what it was like to have a home, and he was out there on his own because of me.

The doorbell rang. "Who in the world could that be?" Hayley asked, her dark eyes sparkling.

I gave her a suspicious look — she had been texting all afternoon with a big smile on her face but wouldn't tell me what was up. I crossed my fingers I wouldn't find a guy in gorilla costume holding a balloon bouquet when I went to answer the door. I didn't. When I opened up, there, standing on the front porch, was Alicia and . . .

"Hugo!" I shrieked, dropping to my knees for a slobbery hello. I threw my arms around him, feeling happy all over. Now I could really celebrate.

Dodge and Gatsby came to the door, greeting Hugo with welcoming wags. Hugo licked a string of cheese off Dodge's face.

"I found the poor guy shivering in an alley yesterday," Alicia explained. "It took forever, but I coaxed him out. I texted Hayley, and she said you might know who he was." She stroked Hugo's broad head. "He's been with me ever since."

I felt my whole body smile. "Really?"

"Really," Alicia beamed. Hugo licked her hand and she crouched down to get closer. "I know, I know!" she cooed, ruffing up the fur on his back. I looked at Dodge. We knew just how they felt. It was puppy love.

"And that's not even the best part," Alicia added. "My parents said I could keep him!" Hugo grunted happily.

"Woof!" Dodge exclaimed.

"Exactly," I agreed. "There's nothing better than a dog and his girl."